Uroboros Saga

BOOK TWO

By Arthur Walker

Cover artwork "Eamon and Abbey" by Arthur Walker
as arranged by Red Couch Creative, Inc.

For Clair

Get updates on my books by following me on Twitter.
@arthurhwalker

FASHION

If we had to run a race together I don't know which of us would win, for if you run fast, I positively gallop; and as for standing still in one place, if it exhausts you, it is bane to me. So let us be off, and as we run we'll talk over our affairs.

DEATH

All right then; and since you are my own mother's child, I hope it will suit you to assist me in my business.

~Leopardi

CHAPTER 1

HELSINKI, FINLAND

10:03 AM, December 31st, 2199

Phelps stared mournfully at outlines of the digital images and inactive objects that populated his virtual workspace. The virtual keyboard flickered slightly in the dim light of his cubical, but his hands were clasped tightly between his knees. He couldn't remember the last time there had been a system outage, let alone on a day like today. Reports were due institution wide and he'd called in sick the day before to play a new video game.

"Phelps, got those reports done yet?" Walter bellowed.

Phelps turned to gaze angrily at Walter, waving to dismiss his desktop. Walter had an annoying habit of just appearing in other people's cubicles like this. It was never funny, not even the first time.

"There's an outage. Do you know what that means?" Phelps said holding his face in his hands.

"Coffee break, that's what it means," Walter said in his perpetually cheerful tone.

Phelps pulled himself up out of his chair and assumed a right hand stance beside Walter as they walked to the break room. This had become their quiet ritual in the past few weeks since Walter's previous office space friend was transferred to Thailand. In spite of Walter's quirks, Phelps was glad for the company as he'd been able to make few friends since he moved to Finland from Los Angeles office.

They rounded the corner into the quiet space of the office reserved for vending machines and the microwaving of whatever one brought from home. Phelps looked up at the automatic espresso machine and scowled, wondering if this would be his last coffee with the firm.

"Don't be like that. It will all turn out. Look at it this way, at least you have an excuse when they come to collect the reports and they aren't finished."

"Walter, there is something wrong in accounting and they can't fix it until I've done my own analysis of our various cash flows. Every time the analytics department walks by my cubical they shoot me daggers."

"With their eyes?"

"No, with their ass," Phelps snapped. "Of course with their eyes. I'm dead, truly and inescapably dead, if I don't get these reports to them by three o'clock today."

"You won't lose your job. Phelps, seriously, what would you do if not this job? We've got all kinds of financial investment points, paid housing, and the mediocre health coverage that's still better than ninety percent of the rest of the world. Would you rather live down than up?"

"I'm thinking about taking night classes in genealogy," Phelps announced, placing his finger provisionally on the caramel and white chocolate button of the coffee machine.

"What? How is that better than what we do? Debt collection is a noble profession," Walter replied in earnest.

"The government agency that regulates us is getting legislation funded that will allow us to collect from people's relatives if they can't pay. I think we'll be able to defund up to second cousins for people who owe money," Phelps stated plainly, rummaging in his pocket for his mobile.

Phelps waved his mobile in front of the automated espresso machine and made his selection. Seconds later, his drink dropped down in a sealed container, steam issuing forth from several pinholes in the top. He waited for a moment for the steam to clear so he wouldn't get burned, then retrieved his beverage.

Walter took his place and quickly made a selection. He then waved his own mobile in front of the automated espresso machine, then checked the display. Forty euros were quickly deducted from his account, the balance displaying momentarily on his mobile. The wall mounted machine was a little slower to push out the second drink, or maybe it just seemed that way after they'd stood here and waited for the same drinks, day after day.

"Dang, forgot to select a flavor. Oh well, plain will have to do. Say, will there be a debtor-deceased clause with this new legislation?" Walter asked while fishing in the bucket for artificial sweetener.

"That's the good news. Companies like ours will be able to resurrect old debts going back to the Global Union Act and defund their living relations," Phelps replied proudly.

"Okay, so why genealogy? That's how this whole conversation got started I think."

"Walter, someone will have to do all the research and at least dummy up the documents to make debt collection claims defensible in court. Genealogists will be in high demand in less than nine months. I figure I could probably get through the first round of night courses in six months and half way through the next by the time the job postings went live," Phelps said blowing on his coffee.

"You think that maybe there are a million other schmucks that thought of the same thing?"

"Hey, you didn't think of it."

"I'm content where I'm at. My debt to income ratio is within alpha taxation parameters, and my kids will end up owing only a couple million to global financing when I retire. I'd call that a win." Walter sipped his coffee and then grimaced as unflavored coffee assaulted his taste buds.

"Seriously? With the face? A little unflavored coffee can't be all that bad."

"Remember when I got sent with extraction division to South America for that big defunding two years ago?"

"You'll never let me forget," Phelps replied, suddenly sorry he'd said anything at all.

"Yeah, well, it was awesome. Anyway, while I was there I had the chance to taste real coffee. When we moved on the cartel's compound they expected me to be there to count ammo used, equipment damaged, and so forth. One of the extraction division guys gave me a sip of some of what he had," Walter related, fond nostalgia overcoming him for a moment.

"Wow, I took the exam, but my eyes weren't good enough to do extraction."

"Phelps, we all took that exam. Who wouldn't want to drop into outlying areas with a gun and take a shot at rogue debtors trying to break the grid?"

"They gave you a gun?" Phelps asked between sips.

"Well no, but I was in a transport with a bunch of guys who had guns."

"You're always adding to the story. So, what did this real coffee taste like?" Phelps said taking the lid off of his own beverage.

"Oh, it was divine. It tasted like a smoky bean, fresh, and roasted, and as if it had been ground up, and distilled in filtered water. Not this synthetic, substandard swill we're used to. I have to have flavoring in it now for it to even be potable," Walter lamented.

"I hate you so much right now," Phelps said with a smile.

Walter was only able to drink half of what he ordered, cursing a little as he poured what remained down the break room sink. Phelps chuckled, his own culinary palette untainted by the good stuff, and able to enjoy the bad. They walked back to the cubical block in silence as cries of exasperation rose up around them.

The office was in disarray as people lamented the loss of productivity and wondered how it would impact their next employee evaluation. Walter and Phelps steered clear of the office busybodies and made their way back to their own division with all haste. The water cooler was completely obscured by worried office workers. Middle management folks leaning in their office doors somewhat frustrated at the outage watched quietly as they contemplated how they would account for the lost productivity.

"Looks like the outage is still plaguing the office," Walter said smiling.

"Oh, do shut up, Walter," Phelps replied shooting him a withering gaze.

Phelps entered his cubical with Walter in tow and stared at his virtual workspace once more. The rendering was flashing now at a slow interval between red and black. Walter scratched his head and looked about for someone from IT.

"They must be on a more important floor trying to fix this," Walter mumbled.

"Odd. Is this not what happens when you've acquired something on credit, such as an appliance, and you allow payment to lapse?" Phelps said tapping the escape key of his virtual keyboard.

"I think so..."

Walter was unable to finish his thought as an automated voice from the building management server intoned a short message over the intercom. "This facility is being defunded. Please exit the building in an orderly fashion. Your compliance is mandatory," the female digitized vocal pattern warned.

"This some kind of drill?" Walter asked as he gathered up his light coat.

"It has to be, or another prank by IT," Phelps grumbled. "They would pull something like this when I have reports due and on the coldest day of the year. Bastards."

There was nothing they could do but head for the exits with the rest of the office drones. Security would be sweeping the building to clear people out within minutes. Walter and Phelps shuffled into the elevator while pulling their coats and scarves tight around their necks. The idea of standing in the Finnish winter for even a half hour while this got sorted only served to darken Phelps' mood.

"I wish I hadn't dumped out my coffee," Walter whispered. "It would have at least served to warm my hands for a bit." His face sagging with sadness.

"Shut up, Walter," Phelps said. The other occupants of the elevator grumbling in unison.

The Helsinki streets were strangely crowded for the time of day. There were a great many people gathered around the entrances to most of the buildings on the block. Phelps paid it no attention as he tried desperately to access his reports using his mobile.

"It looks like the entire financial district just exited their offices," Walter said pointing.

Marjorie, the analytics manager, wandered up to where Phelps and Walter stood and smiled weakly. She was dressed somewhat more warmly than they were, sporting a long coat with a hood and fur fringe. Phelps hid his face with his hand in a gesture of avoidance, he already knew what she was going to ask.

"I don't suppose you'll be getting those reports done by three?" she asked.

Walter laughed for a moment until Phelps shot him a deadly glance.

"Marjorie, I will try and get to my employee account with my mobile and finish them out here in the cold if that's what it takes," Phelps replied.

"Good man. Truman from accounting keeps using it as an excuse to come into the executive workspace and flirt with me," Marjorie said scowling.

"That's the guy with the mole, and the Slavic accent?" Walter asked as he rubbed his hands together in the cold.

"Uh, yeah. He did give me this really nice coat, though. Unrequited office crushes are not without perks I suppose," Marjorie said, continuing to maintain her scowl.

"He's from Bulgaria from what I understand. His mother and father are quite wealthy, owning a great many yak farms and turnip plantations. The only reason he maintains employment is to look for a wife with wide hips and a work ethic," Phelps said as deadpan as possible.

"Liar. If only that were true," Marjorie said pinching Phelps on the arm as savagely as she could.

"There's only one way to find out if I'm right," Phelps joked rubbing his now bruised arm.

"Even if it were the end of the world, Truman would still get the brush off from me. His ears are hair factories," Marjorie whispered.

"What was that, Marjorie?" Walter asked.

"Nothing."

They shivered in the snow for several minutes, waiting for someone to tell them they could go back inside. The cold was unrelenting, and people began to congregate around the huge industrial exhaust systems in the alleys between buildings. Snow continued to fall slowly in the windless air as the street filled with the sounds of confused business people wondering what was going on.

"Walter, how's your kid doing in soccer?" Phelps said finally, trying to ignore the cold.

"Oh, not well. His notice of qualification came late. We wanted him to be able to play so we decided to go forward with the gene therapy before getting the blood tests back." His voice wavered as he shivered in the cold.

"Growths?" Marjorie ventured.

"Yeah, even had one on the face. The doctors tell you there's only a one percent chance of mutation, so we figured the blood tests were a formality,"

"Your kid has the worst luck," Phelps said, chuckling.

"It's true, but how could we know he was a member of the one percent? They removed the growths, and were able to use nanoid machine rebuilders to evoke a higher degree of healing to limit scarring. Still, I think we'll skip school pictures this year," Walter said checking his mobile.

"Sorry to hear that," Marjorie said, feeling a little bad for asking.

"It's okay. The doctors let little Roger keep one of the growths in a jar of fluid. It wriggles about in there, even weeks later. Totally freaks out my wife, but Roger has been working extra hard on his biology homework. Says he wants to be a scientist when he grows up," Walter replied halfheartedly.

"Scientist? The pay decent?" Phelps murmured, his face already numb from the cold.

"Yeah, if you get to work with Metasapients. Y'know, tailored humanoids for hazardous duty? They had a Metasapient that worked on the lunar colony come into his school, an Ichthyic variety that had to wear a bowl on its head. It was a human-fish genetic hybrid designed to work in the fluid exchange systems on the colony," Walter explained, holding up his mobile in a vain attempt to get a better signal.

"Problems with your mobile, Walter?" Phelps asked, still wrestling with his own.

"Yeah, it dropped me from the corporate private network to the old auxiliary public."

Marjorie pulled hers out and gazed at the small screen while Phelps tentatively tapped at his own.

"Mine's the same."

"Mine, too."

"Looks like everyone is having the same problem," Walter observed, looking out at the dozens of faces in the street illuminated by the glow of their mobiles.

"So much for using my mobile to download the reports and finish them. It'll take hours on the old auxiliary public," Phelps whined.

There was an ominous boom in the distance. It sounded like a loud drum being struck from the top of one of the hills along the skyline beyond the city. Everyone on the street turned their heads and looked for a moment, before returning their attention to their mobiles. A second later, the windows of the buildings around them rattled softly.

"What is going on? Are they going to let us back in?" Marjorie complained.

Security was out in the street, having cleared the building, their yellow parkas glistening as snow melted across their shoulders. A moment later, the sound of a crash issued forth from the parking garage, as if there'd been a fender bender. The noise from the crowd picked up as the digital monitor over the building entrance gave off a single tone, the type that usually preceded an announcement by the building maintenance server.

Walter and Phelps looked back at the entrance just as the blast doors on the reinforced building slid shut, then the activity light above the door turned from green to red. A similar sound could be heard up and down the street as office buildings, shopping centers, and espresso cart windows closed. It was not an unfamiliar sight after the terrorist attack drill earlier last year. The global financial division shut the entire city down for an hour as part of a preparedness initiative, but that was in the summer.

"Phelps, is it possible that debt collections has been defunded?" Walter asked looking back at the entrance.

"There are supposed to be safeguards, and we're regulated and fall under several legislative umbrellas. I struggle to contemplate how we could be defunded," Phelps said, his voice tainted by his irritation.

Angry cries and moans of exasperation rose up from the crowd. As the mob of frustrated employees surged for the door, several people got upended. Somewhere, a coffee cup clattered to the ground. The air seemed to grow colder and the snow fell a little more persistently.

The crowd parted to allow a small vehicle and a passenger to get through. A Canine Metasapient 'law dog' rolled up on an ATV fully armed, an unusual sight in Helsinki. She was taller than your average human and covered in white fur that got considerably longer as it grew from the top of her head. She had keen, crystal blue eyes that scanned the crowd tirelessly. A lump rose in Phelps' throat at the sight of her.

The Metasapient gave a loud bark in response to several men and women in business casual banging on the door of an office building across the street. A few people complied, but most displayed the usual disdain for tailored life forms. She barked again. Those close enough to her clutched at their ears and grimaced in pain.

"Rioting and property damage is forbidden. Your compliance with civic edicts is mandatory," she growled loudly enough to be heard over the noise of the crowd.

Phelps harbored no love for Metasapients, but the canine-human hybrid might have a clue as to what was going on. He wondered where all the human police officers were as he walked up to talk to the law dog. Walter, almost compelled by habit, followed along behind.

"Where are we going?" Walter asked.

"I'm going to ask the law dog if it... she, whatever, knows what's going on," Phelps snapped, growing more irritated with the situation.

The law dog stepped off her ATV and barked again at several people trying in vain to get into their personal vehicles in the parking lot. She turned to meet Phelps' gaze, panting slightly in the cold air. The coloration of her fur and blue eyes betrayed her as one of the members of the Nordic Patrol that usually patrolled outlying areas. Most of the canine Metasapients employed by the Metropolitan Police were black or brown in their coloration, and didn't carry as many weapons.

"Officer, what's going on?" Phelps asked angrily.

"Please remain calm, sir" the law dog responded, her oddly husky voice tinged with the accent of someone trained to speak by a computer.

"I'm trying, but we're all freezing and the buildings appear to be defunded with all occupants evicted. How is that possible?"

"You appear to be someone employed in the financial industry, I would ask you the same," the law dog responded.

"I don't like your tone," Phelps responded.

The law dog stepped conspicuously into Phelps' personal bubble so that he could feel her breath on his face. She paused for a moment, looming over the top of him. Phelps swallowed and straightened his tie as he averted his eyes from her gaze.

"Local precincts have been defunded. I came down from the hills because I haven't been served notice of termination yet. Technically, I don't have to be here, but I'm not the sort to just watch idly while you people freeze to death," the law dog responded, her sharp teeth appearing from behind her black lips.

"How did you get here so fast?" Phelps asked. "The building was defunded only minutes ago."

"Whatever is going on hit poorer outlying areas first and has been spreading toward wealthier parts of town since very early morning," the law dog replied.

Phelps looked down at the ground somewhat ashamed.

"How can we help?" Walter asked.

"Start pulling the tops off of trash bins and drag them to sheltered areas. I'll use the flares I have to start barrel fires. They should burn for 24 hours. Hopefully emergency response will arrive before the sun goes down," the law dog growled.

"What's your name, Officer?" Marjorie asked.

"Abbey," the law dog replied.

It took them a half hour to prep the trash bins along the roads of the financial district as Abbey went around dropping the few flares she had into them. Phelps and his two coworkers tried in vain to contact their homes, and then went down to check and see if the metro was running. The tunnels were quiet, illuminated by emergency lighting only.

As they walked back toward their office they could see people trying in vain to access their personal vehicles. Each had a small red light blinking on the dash indicating that the vehicle was to be collected for non-payment by a repossession agent. Some of the cars had sustained damage either from frustration or desperation to recover items from the interior. Ironically, on the walk back, they saw at least one recovery agent standing by his defunded tow truck awaiting collection as well.

The financial district was a strange sight. Brokers and accountants clustered around the barrel fires as Abbey patrolled the length of the street to maintain a tenuous degree of order as tempers flared and frustration mounted. The cold didn't help as some people had left the office without their coats thinking the whole affair was merely a drill.

"Marjorie, was there any indication that the global trade market was in some sort of trouble?" Phelps ventured.

"Not when I checked my retirement package yesterday morning. Everything appeared normal."

"Feh, I never look at my package," Walter replied as cheerfully as he could muster.

"With that gut, I'm not surprised," Phelps quipped.

Marjorie pinched Phelps, harder than the last time.

"Ow!" Phelps exclaimed as he rubbed his arm. "How is it you found the exact place you pinched me previously?"

"They made me head of the department for just that reason. I'm good at corralling you morons. You all need to quit picking on Walter, he might be your boss someday," Marjorie said somewhat disgusted.

"Really?" Walter asked, his eyes lighting up.

"No, but it was the most terrifying threat I could make," Marjorie replied with a wink.

"No respect for the short guy. Okay, let's see if the law dog has heard anything," Walter said, his cheerful demeanor fading as he self-consciously looked down at his protruding stomach.

Abbey put her radio away as the trio approached, smiling as professionally as she could.

"Officer, have you heard anything? Emergency response on their way?" Marjorie asked, rubbing her arms for warmth.

"No. Civil communications went down ten minutes ago. Just previous to that there were reports of looting and unrest in the commercial districts. People were trying to break into shopping centers that had been defunded. Last I heard, members of my own Nordic Patrol were trying to rescue homeowners who had been trapped in the ventilation systems of their own homes. They'd been locked out and tried to get back inside. I don't know what's going on, but it is city wide," Abbey said, her long pointed ears standing erect as if trying to detect some faraway sound.

"Well, if they can't contact you, they can't terminate you either," Walter said cheerfully.

"Shut up, Walter," Marjorie and Phelps said in unison.

Abbey looked upward into the sky, her razor sharp teeth protruding slightly as her lips parted. She closed her eyes for a moment and raised her hand as if to ask for silence. The three were quiet for only that moment, trying to hear whatever it was Abbey could hear. At last, Abbey opened her cold blue eyes, her semi-professional smile vanishing as she started her ATV.

"What is it?" Walter asked, knowing that Metasapients had enhanced senses.

"I can hear people screaming in terror, faintly. It doesn't make sense, but it sounds like it's coming from above us. Maybe people trapped in the upper levels of the buildings? I can't imagine what would elicit such a response from them..." Abbey whispered, her rigid mind trying to lock onto what the sounds meant.

"Dear God," Walter cried.

"What?" Phelps said, shaking Walter by the shoulders.

"Commercial transports, with thousands of people aboard... what if the airlines were defunded in mid-flight?!" Walter exclaimed.

"There are safeguards..." Marjorie began, just as a commercial transport broke the clouds above them.

They all gazed up at the transport, awestruck. Its hulking metallic mass was devoid of illumination, the usual array of safety lighting completely dark, as were every tiny passenger window and the cockpit. It seemed to fall in slow motion, gliding down at a dangerously steep angle. A collective sound of exclamation went up from the crowd as people pointed. The sound was quickly replaced by cries of panic and screams as the thrum of footfalls filled the streets.

"Run," Abbey growled, gunning the engine of her four-wheeler.

Phelps broke into a panicked run as the crowd surged around him. He lost sight of Marjorie and Walter as they hesitated and got knocked down by the stampede of brokers, analysts, and finance consultants. Wingtips and high heels trampled anything and anyone unfortunate enough to get in their way as the commercial transport plummeted toward the Anderson Central Credit Bureau building.

The transport hit the reinforced structure with such force that it flattened everyone down below, knocking them prone. As it broke apart, the internal electronics within the transport sparked, igniting the aviation propellant that had once resided within now shattered fuel tanks. Fire, tons of sundered metal, and hundreds of burning corpses rained down on the crowd below. Driven by fear, those uninjured in the crowd regained their feet and resumed trampling the dead and injured in their ardent desire to flee the scene.

Abbey, standing atop her ATV, barked at the crowd in vain trying to restore order as cries for help ringing in her ears were silenced by thudding foot falls. She leapt into the crowd swinging her tactical baton in a wide arc, her powerful arms battering the cubical slaves to the ground. She strode forward, using her weight to her advantage. She reached down and picked up an injured child. She had a temporary wrist band that betrayed her as a recent resident of one of the corporate daycare centers nearby.

A couple of men from the crowd, indignant from being knocked down, stood up and lunged at Abbey. She yielded to her training, drawing and discharging her sidearm in one fluid movement. Each of the men took a round, center of mass, and fell backward. The crowd around her recoiled in horror at first, then responded with fury. She was just a Metasapient, her life wasn't worth even a tenth of a human life by societal standards. She was just property by most established laws.

Abbey didn't care anymore; her job was to restore order. She leveled her sidearm menacingly at the crowd and let loose a low growl, her powerful maternal instinct making her momentarily irrational as the child she cradled in her arm struggled to breath with broken ribs. The crowd began to hurl bottles and burning debris at Abbey as she retreated to her ATV. She pistol whipped a man wearing an expensive suit off the back of her ride, even as he struggled to figure out how to operate it.

"I'm sorry, sir, but you aren't authorized to operate this vehicle. Law enforcement only," Abbey barked, as the suit made a hasty retreat.

Phelps struggled to push his way through the crowd to where he last saw Marjorie and Walter. As he got close he watched passively as Abbey shot and killed two men lunging at her.

"Idiots," he grunted as he looked about the ground for his coworkers.

Walter was more or less where he'd left him, cradling Marjorie in his arms as she bled out in the snow. She'd been trampled, puncture wounds from designer shoes oozed blood across her abdomen and she struggled to breathe. Walter himself was bloodied and bruised, but his girth seemed to insulate him somewhat from the reckless assault of the panicked crowd.

"Officer Abbey!" Phelps shouted.

The law dog turned, her fur flecked with blood, eyes full of unbridled fury.

"Please, my boss is hurt. Please, help us," he pleaded.

Abbey's strong instinct to protect the humans overcame her rage, and she turned her ATV around and rode over. She panted heavily as she handed the small girl to Phelps to hold while she knelt down next to Marjorie. Walter sat back slightly so Abbey could sniff Marjorie's wounds.

"Her digestive tract is punctured, and so is her stomach by the scent of the blood rising up. Unless you can get her to a hospital, it might be more merciful to let her bleed out than suffer the pain of her body poisoning itself," Abbey growled, turning a murderous gaze toward the crowd.

"No. We have to do something," Walter cried, tears freezing to his face.

Phelps turned and looked back toward the skyline as two more commercial transports began making a slow descent to the ground just to their side of the hills. The girl in his arms gasped for air, her small jacket wholly insufficient to keep her warm. Phelps took off his own light jacket and wrapped it around the unconscious little girl.

"What could have happened to cause this?" Walter muttered as he tried in vain to make Marjorie more comfortable.

"Global market failure outside of legislative safeguards," Phelps responded grimly.

Abbey grabbed the shotgun from its locking point on her ATV and thumbed several shells into the ammo tube. She ran a round into the chamber and another shell into the tube for good measure. Phelps looked on nervously, Abbey's ears twitching in different directions as she took in the sounds and probably the smells around her.

"People are already in full panic-mode. A woman was just beat to death two blocks away for her sack lunch," Abbey growled.

"Dear God," Walter exclaimed.

"What do you intend to do?" Phelps said, laying the small girl beside Marjorie inside her long coat.

"I'm going to do my job. I'm going to try to keep the peace. Hopefully there are more Nordic Patrol officers already doing the same," Abbey replied, putting her hand reflexively to the silver badge pinned to her tactical vest.

Phelps looked out across the flaming wreckage and at the dozens of bodies lying in the street, and at the terrified people huddled around barrel fires and fading heating vents. His mind reeled, his sanity sitting at the precipice between rational thought and sheer terror. Everything around him was unreal and dreamlike.

"Walter, find us a couple of coats. Pull them off corpses if you have to," Phelps said, his voice calm.

"What?" Walter mumbled, his gaze firmly fixed on the ground.

"Abbey will need our help, even with a badge and a gun. She'll need some humans to back her up. Most people don't see her the way I do now," Phelps explained.

"And how is that exactly?" Abbey snarled.

"As our best chance to survive this situation. You can't do this alone, and if the rest of the Nordic Patrol has deserted their posts, I'd hesitate to think of what some of the anti-Metasapient bigots around here might try to do to you. Even you have to sleep," Phelps replied, trying to make Marjorie and the little girl more comfortable.

Abbey stood there for a moment in contemplation. Her rigid and inflexible mind began to throw off some of the shackles of her ingrained desire to conform and obey the training she had received. Technically, she wasn't allowed to work beside humans, only take orders from them. However, her first order of business was to see to the protection of humanity, and if working with them would help her achieve that end, the other rules seemed frivolous.

Walter came back over with a handful of coats, some were singed while others were bloody. They quietly divvied them up and layered them on as best as they could. Walter looked down at Marjorie and the little girl as shock began to set in. They spasmed and shivered as their bodies began to shut down from their injuries, blood loss, and the cold. He couldn't help but think they might be the lucky ones.

"What do we do now?" Walter asked.

Phelps turned to Abbey.

"We... we should find a place to act as our base. Somewhere old and unfortified that isn't subject to foreclosure lockdown. There will be nowhere in the Helsinki core that is like that. If we can't find a place like that, we might have to go below the city to the tunnels and ask the Drones for sanctuary," Abbey said, thinking out loud.

"Drones? You mean those genetically engineered sub-humans actually exist?" Walter stammered.

"I suppose I'm a sub-human too?" Abbey said looking at Walter disdainfully.

"Gosh, no," Walter replied somewhat diminished.

"They are real, but after the project that produced them was defunded some years back, they remained underground tapping into the water and power of the cities above. As long as they don't cause trouble, the Central Global Government has allowed them to persist. Most of the colonies continued to perform their function in the tunnels and help maintain the city infrastructure, blissfully unaware their corporate masters had all but forgotten them," Abbey replied, pulling her long white hair back into a ponytail.

"How do you know all this?" Phelps asked.

Abbey just stared at Phelps for a moment, making it clear his question wasn't receiving an answer.

"What if people try to force their way into the underground homes of the Drones? Surely, there are other people who are aware of them," Phelps said, somewhat exasperated.

"Anyone with civil service experience or employment with Helsinki Metro might have an inkling of their existence. There are dark zones in the underground grid you are instructed to avoid because Drones are sometimes dangerous and territorial. A few Type One Drones are active in Helsinki," Abbey said, checking the fuel level of her ATV.

"Dangerous? Type One?" Walter replied, wringing his hands in worry.

"Type One Drones were created for hazardous environments, and military duty. Even Type Two law enforcement grade Metasapients, such as myself, have something to fear from Type One Drones. It is not just for their physical and sensory enhancements, but for the training they receive in the manufacturing cells that birthed them," Abbey remarked, doing little to throw salve on Walter's fears.

"Are they automatically hostile?" Phelps asked, suddenly curious.

"No. Type One Drones have generally seen enough extra vehicular activity and off-world combat that they tend to avoid bloodshed. A few are flawed, and the aberrant ones are relentless killers whose only instinct is to fight. I haven't heard of one in Helsinki, though," Abbey said.

"You sound like you've actually met a Type One," Walter observed.

Abbey started up her ATV and rode along slowly while Phelps and Walter followed. Walter turned and looked back over his shoulder at Marjorie and the small girl as they disappeared in the distance. It seemed heartless to leave them behind, but there was nothing they could do. Every hospital would likely be defunded, and each was likely fortified to meet the Central Global Government's anti-insurgency standards to repel terrorist attacks. Once the doors closed, no one without a Central Global Government, or CGG alpha level clearance or higher would be getting inside.

The streets beyond the financial district were peppered with debris. There were groups of people attempting to garner warmth from a fire or exhaust vent at the side of a building. There was also the occasional dead body. Most didn't appear to be the result of falling commercial transports or stampeding crowds. They were the victims of random crimes of passion or desperation.

Phelps periodically checked his mobile. The old auxiliary public network was clogged with desperate attempts by people to reach loved ones, offers to trade expensive luxury items for food or water, and pleas from people trapped inside defunded buildings and complexes. Worse, the messages came from all over Finland and the surrounding areas. Whatever was going on wasn't just restricted to Helsinki.

Abbey stopped to render aid to an elderly couple who appeared to be in distress. Someone had knocked them down and taken their wallets and their mobiles. It looked like they had been out for a walk and were properly dressed, hiding under a bridge near a public terminal after being unsuccessful at using it to garner aid. Abbey tried to explain to them that the civic works network and all associated channels were down and that they should go home and wait for instructions from the CGG.

Phelps couldn't help but wonder if those instructions were forthcoming, or if national emergency services were even operable. If hospitals and police stations could be defunded, anything probably could. In the wake of the CGG's anti-insurgency standards, most government buildings, hospitals, and other physical edifices of public works were fortified and subject to foreclosure and eviction lockdown. It was supposed to be a measure to force local governments to avoid overspending.

"Well, there is an upside to this, Phelps," Walter commented while they waited for Abbey to finish reassuring the elderly couple.

"I'm almost afraid to ask," Phelps replied, rolling his eyes.

"You probably don't need to worry about getting those reports in by three o'clock."

"Walter, do shut up."

CHAPTER 2

RURAL AREA NEAR HELSINKI, FINLAND

5:33 AM December 31st, 2199

Ezra's War Journal, Part 4

I awoke at my post having dozed off. Thankfully, no one had attempted to approach the cabin during the night and all seemed peaceful. It was bitterly cold and the winter clothes I had managed to scrounge together did little to protect me. I could only imagine what the people in the city just over the hills went through yesterday.

Our cabin was ancient, built before most synthetic materials became mandatory and was warmer, stronger, and better in many ways as a consequence. Still, I preferred the basement when I wasn't keeping an eye on things. There was a room that looked to have been set up for a child, with a small bed that was just my size.

I could still see smoke trailing up into the sky to intermingle with ever darkening clouds. A big snow storm seemed imminent and the wind was already beginning to grow stronger. I dropped from my perch beneath the roofline of the cabin to the snow below and began walking the perimeter to see if we'd been followed.

It was still too soon to see people walking in from the metropolis. Nevertheless, those with transportation would be looking for food and shelter off-grid. Some might be innocent people trying to survive, but many would be ruthless looters. I had ceased to be amazed by a human's ability to go from being noble benefactor to soulless scavenger.

Silverstein met me around the back, axe in hand.

"I'm going to chop some more wood. Taylor is still sleeping, but she seems to be a little bit better than last night. You can actually see her breathing now," he reported.

"There's a storm coming, and depending on when the snow begins to fall, we can probably expect company from the city beyond those hills," I whispered, checking my rifle for the fourth time.

"Helsinki is the city you're talking about. It was one of the most modern in the world which means that there will be very few vehicles in town that wouldn't have been put out of commission by the shutdown. From the smoke, some commercial transports must have gone down when the airlines and shipping companies were defunded. I bet today was a really bad day," Silverstein replied, casting his gaze to the horizon.

"We've enough food for weeks in the cabin, especially if I only eat when I absolutely have to," I said.

"How often it that?"

"I can get by with a small amount of food once a week or so. I won't be at a one hundred percent in a fight, but hopefully the snow storm precludes such for a while."

Silverstein nodded his agreement and set about chopping wood. I was still tired, but I decided I needed to keep an eye on things a while longer. Until the sun began to set in the early afternoon, all was silent save for a few gunshots in the distance.

We stayed at the cabin for two weeks while Taylor recovered. During that time, I kept a constant vigil over the area around our shelter and dug many snow caves as it piled up higher and higher with each storm. Never having been to Finland, I couldn't be sure if this was natural for the time of year or not.

One morning I caught Silverstein standing in the bathroom looking in the mirror at himself. He looked ancient, his skin wrinkled and coarse, and his posture stooped over as though he was struggling to carry his weight. He turned towards me and I watched awestruck as he suddenly began to get more and more youthful until he appeared as I remembered him.

"Whoa," I exclaimed.

"Yeah, I've been slowly figuring out how to do it while we've been here," Silverstein reported, somewhat embarrassed.

"You can make yourself appear young or old at will?"

Silverstein began to rapidly change, becoming even more youthful until he appeared as a pre-teen version of himself. I could only blink in astonishment. Silverstein laughed mirthfully at my apparent surprise.

"I haven't fully explored the limits yet, but my mind and memories seem unaffected. I'd hoped maybe this would aid me in remembering my past, but I'm as confused as I ever was," Silverstein squeaked, his youthful voice cracking in the middle of his sentence.

"It's a very strange ability. I've heard of humans with interesting mutations, but this takes the cake. When I was being trained in the factory as a Droneling, there was a psychic who could read minds," I stated, still somewhat amazed by what I'd seen.

Silverstein slowly assumed his more familiar mid-twenties look and straightened out his shirt. Taylor came down the hallway in a colorful nightgown she'd sewn together, presumably the night before. It was fuzzy in some places and just smooth fabric in others. I was transfixed.

"Like it?" Taylor said, striking a pose.

Silverstein smiled and shook his head.

"Where did you get the material to make that monstrous thing?" he asked with a chuckle.

"It's not monstrous! It's cute. Anyway, someone with a timeshare for this place had kids. One of the rooms in the basement had a trash bag full of stuffed animals. I took them all apart and made me a fuzzy-snuzzy to sleep in," Taylor replied, somewhat indignant.

"I think it's marvelous," I said reaching out to pet Taylor's shoulder.

We retreated to the front room for some warmth and some twice-made tea. I began to nurse a powerful envy of Taylor's fuzzy-snuzzy as she called it. She looked very cozy, and for some reason, I couldn't seem to get warm. I had a strange sense all of a sudden that we weren't alone, but the smell of the fire in the wood stove was all I could detect.

"Is that a bear in a bulletproof vest?" Taylor said pointing out the window from her vantage point.

I leapt to my feet scooping up my rifle. I gazed out the window and saw a huge bear making its way through the snow. It appeared to be outfitted in a tactical harness of some sort, and it was heavily armed. For a moment, I was very afraid because of its size. Marshaling my courage, I stepped out the front door and leveled my rifle.

"Stop! You're trespassing!" I bellowed as Silverstein and Taylor pressed in behind me.

The bear stopped and looked up at me, cocking one snow encrusted eyebrow in my direction. It rose up revealing that it wasn't just any bear, but an Ursine Metasapient. He had a silver star pinned to his chest, several satchels of supplies, and a medical kit.

"Point the peashooter somewhere else. I'm a member of the Nordic Patrol. I'm just going cabin to cabin doing welfare checks," the bear roared in response.

"He's a cop?" Taylor whispered, somewhat astonished.

"Looks that way," Silverstein said squinting out into the snow.

I lowered my weapon and stepped out where the Metasapient officer could see me. It was clear he'd never seen a Drone before, and while I'd never seen a bear Metasapient, we instantly knew what each other was because of our genetic programming.

"Hey, soldier. Get some of that tea you're brewing?" the officer called out.

"You'll have to come to the garage, you're too big for the front door," I replied.

He lumbered through the snow effortlessly toward the garage which I opened for him from the inside. He stepped, snow piling up on the concrete around him as it fell from his body. He shook abruptly causing Taylor to squeal gleefully as cold water went everywhere.

"Sorry, sometimes I do that out of instinct without consideration to who else might be about," the officer said, brushing the last of the snow from his shoulders.

I closed the garage and opened a vent so that some of the heat from the wood stove would filter down to the garage. It'd been weeks since we'd seen anyone, and the officer might be able to tell us some of what was going on in the surrounding area. Silverstein handed him a cup of tea that looked comically small when clutched between the bear's enormous paw-like hands.

"So, Officer..." Silverstein began.

"Eamon, that's the name the factory gave me. I like it," the officer replied, taking a sip of the tea.

"Officer Eamon, can you tell us what you've seen lately when you've been about on your patrols?" I asked, before Silverstein could get out another word.

"You're a Drone, right? Not from around here?" he replied.

"Right."

"Well, usually when we get snow like this, the hills are alive with people doing Nordic skiing. The cabins fill up and I don't have to go far for something hot to drink. People treat my kind better out here than they do in the city," Officer Eamon said between sips.

Taylor could only stare, doing her best not to laugh at the sight of the huge bear as he gingerly sipped his tea, making it last as long as he could. Silverstein and I did our best to explain why the people probably hadn't come up to the cabins. Officer Eamon seemed genuinely distressed that the people in the city might be in trouble. Metasapients are designed and bred to be naturally protective of humans.

"I came across a couple along the highway that looked to have frozen to death. I tried to call it in and I left a cadaver marker so they would get picked up when the plows went by. I thought it was odd that I couldn't find their vehicle. Poor souls must have been trying to walk somewhere from Helsinki when the storm hit," Officer Eamon said, his fuzzy face contorting to display deep sadness.

"The man responsible, Dr. Madmar, used a transport to escape the military facility a few miles from here. Have you seen any downed air vehicles?" Silverstein asked.

"No. I've been in the deep wilderness for the last month," Officer Eamon said. "I had some time off coming to me, so I grabbed my rifles and went hunting. I haven't talked to command for weeks. I can't believe this all happened while I was gone."

"Are there others like you?" Taylor said smiling as she petted Officer Eamon's huge fuzzy arm.

"I'm the only Ursine, but there are many Canine units deployed by the Nordic Patrol. I haven't seen any lately though. Haven't even come across their scent which isn't odd because we rarely overlap preferring to each have our own territory."

"Could you guide us back to Helsinki?" Silverstein asked.

"Easily, but it'll take three or four days depending on the weather, and it's a little cold outside if you hadn't noticed," Officer Eamon quipped.

"I'll be okay with my coats and my fuzzy-snuzzy," Taylor said pulling her multicolored cloak of stuffed animal death more tightly about her shoulders.

"I'm concerned that in the weeks since the shutdown, people in the city will have given themselves to barbarism and worse to survive. Getting to the city will be hard, but I'm more worried about what we'll find," Silverstein lamented.

The officer considered Silverstein's words while he stirred what remained of his tea.

"Sounds like incentive for me to go back. My brothers and sisters who are still on patrol will have their hands full," Officer Eamon said, just before downing the rest of the tea.

"Why is there only one Ursine? You are so big, and you obviously care about people," Taylor asked.

"Ma'am, where are you from?"

"Port Montaigne."

"I lived in North America for a few years after my training at the factory. There were a lot of Metasapients on the job, but we couldn't do our job and protect the populace because they wouldn't protect us. Some low-life guns a Metasapient down, it's considered a property crime. Over here, the laws aren't that different, but the people are. When I worked in Helsinki, I could always tell who was from around here and who was a transplant by more than their accent. It was how they treated me and my brothers and sisters that wore a badge. There are human police officers, but they are all administrators. Most have forgotten what it means to do this job, and why we do it," Officer Eamon began.

"There are hardly any Metasapients where I come from, I guess that explains why," Taylor said.

"Two years ago, there was a group of armed robbers that delighted in killing innocent people, particularly on camera. Their real weapon wasn't their guns, it was the fear they spread. They worked mainly in Denmark until the CGG deployed a Custodian to try and deal with them. They fled to Finland where they ran into me," Officer Eamon continued.

Silverstein and I exchanged looks, knowing something of how these stories can end.

"They were in Stanley & Travis Traders Bank during the busiest time of day. While we were putting together a perimeter, they shot a little girl and pushed her body out the front door on the steps."

"Oh my God, what did you do?" Taylor asked, horrified.

"I went into the bank and put a stop to them. They shot me up real bad. The people inside the bank never forgot what I did to those guys. Even though I was the only one hurt in the exchange, it was a media circus and police watchdog groups had a field day. They said it proved that Ursine Metasapients were unpredictable and too dangerous for urban use. Every other Ursine working Metro transferred out of the country or into the rural patrols. After I healed up, it didn't take too long until I was the only one in Finland."

"I'm sorry," Taylor said, somewhat remorseful for asking.

"It's okay, I like this better. The people who live out here are glad I'm around and no one bothers me anymore. My only regret is that I didn't go into the bank sooner. That little girl might still be alive," Officer Eamon said.

Taylor gazed mournfully at Officer Eamon, her eyes brimming with tears.

"Hard to get a date now, though," Officer Eamon joked.

Taylor smiled, but I could see that both she and Silverstein were deeply disturbed by the story. Having endured discrimination for being different myself, I marveled at how easy Officer Eamon had gotten off. They'd have 'retired' him if he'd done something like that in North America.

"I can take you to the city as soon as you're ready to go. Make sure you bring a little extra food," Officer Eamon winked.

We did our best to prepare for the journey. I didn't ask why Silverstein thought we should go, but it was doing us no good hunkered down in the cabin, and our food wouldn't last forever. Officer Eamon was probably our best chance to get out of there. Still, I was cold, like I had never been before. I couldn't understand it because I'd swam in freezing water displaced from refrigerant tanks in the sewer tunnels back home.

I wore every bit of kid's clothing I could find in the place that would fit my slender frame. Silverstein loaded up a sled with supplies and covered them with a tarp while Taylor picked up and tested every battery we had. Officer Eamon shifted his own load so that his modified firearms were more easily accessible in case there was trouble. I marveled at the craftsmanship of his weapons, each with grips and a modified trigger guard to accommodate his gigantic paw-hands. They were Euro-zone in make, and chambered with heavy ammunition I was unfamiliar with. They looked like they were for taking down vehicles and small aircraft and not intended to be used on people.

We finished off our morning tea and set out into the snow in the afternoon. We followed along behind Officer Eamon as he cut a swath through the snow. He was frighteningly strong, acting like a small plow ahead of us. Occasionally, he would turn his broad head around to gaze at us and make sure we were still there. I lagged behind as the cold seemed to make my limbs heavier and heavier.

Finally, Officer Eamon stopped and doubled back to where I was barely standing.

"You okay there, Ezra?" he inquired, trying not to injure my dignity.

"I'm fine," I replied, leaning heavily on my rifle.

"My eyes are getting kind of tired, maybe you ought to sit on my shoulder for a bit and help me keep watch," he replied.

"Oh, that is so unfair," Taylor said smiling.

Officer Eamon picked me up and put me on his huge shoulder where I sat and shivered doing my best to keep an eye out. I must have fallen asleep because the next thing I knew I was laying in the sled all covered up. Someone had made a fire and I was being offered a broth. I drank it and felt a little better.

"Don't know anything about Drones, and I've never seen one before," Officer Eamon said, sipping his own broth from a bowl dwarfed by his paws.

"They were commissioned by the CGG decades ago for hazardous work below ground when certain cities became too big for their own infrastructure. Because some of it was so old and buried so very deep, they allowed genetic experimentation to produce a race of workers to that end. At least that's what the public knows about them," Silverstein said, poking the fire.

"Officer Eamon, Ezra is special," Taylor said patting my head. "He's Type One and a pygmy."

"Pygmy? Makes sense, I always thought Drones were the same size as humans, or a little smaller maybe. Oh, and just call me Eamon, we're all friends here."

We all nodded, glad to dispense with the formality.

"Never really thought about it until now. I've met Type Two, Three, Four, and Five Metasapients. They have a similar range of Drones?" Eamon asked.

"No. There are only Type One, Three, Five and Six Drones. No Type Two or Fours," I replied feebly.

"Type Six?"

"Psychics. I've met a couple of Type Six Drones from Ezra's hive, commune, family, whatever," Silverstein said as he got me a second helping of broth.

"So, they live in collectives?" Eamon asked.

"Yeah, they don't wander about by themselves like you do. Ezra appears to be the exception," Taylor said patting my head again.

"Maybe he isn't," Eamon replied, looking over at me deeply concerned.

Silverstein and Taylor looked at each other and shrugged, then looked to me.

"I don't know what he's talking about," I squeaked, still feeling impossibly weak and cold.

"There are Chiroptera Metasapients in Mexico and South America. They were designed to act in groups and if any one of them get separated from the others for too long, they'll get sick and eventually die, presumably from loneliness," Eamon said sniffing me.

"Chiroptera?" Taylor asked.

"Bats," Silverstein said, wiggling his fingers at Taylor like fleshy spider limbs.

"You guys are totally making this up just to freak me out," Taylor said folding her arms.

"Wish I was. Hopefully we can find some Drones in Helsinki to commune with your friend, or at least give us some insight into what's wrong with him," Officer Eamon said putting his paw reassuringly on my chest.

The next day was rough. It began to snow again and while I felt a little bit better I couldn't help but wonder if Eamon was right. I felt this strange loneliness that seemed to pervade my entire being and my dreams were filled with anxious flashes of my home beneath Port Montaigne. I desperately wanted to know how the others were doing and was deathly afraid of forgetting their faces.

We climbed, crested, and descended down the backside of forested hill after forested hill. I couldn't figure out how the old bear knew where he was going. He never even stopped to ponder where he was or look at the sky. He just seemed to know where to go. Then as it was starting to get dark, Eamon hesitated just before cresting a hill, his large ears twitching slightly.

He pulled his rifle from its place on his harness and rushed to the top of the hill. Silverstein, Taylor, and I trudged upward behind him and went over the top as quickly as we could. I could hear Eamon's deafeningly loud voice over the wind and snowfall clearly as he drew the slide back on his rifle.

"Stop! Armed Nordic Enforcement, cease and desist, you are under arrest!"

I squinted through the snow at what looked like a Snowcat, painted bright orange, a trail left in its wake indicating that it probably came from wherever we were going. Arrayed around it were several men with guns who had pulled a couple of groups of people from the vehicle. There were men, women, and children kneeling in the snow. The armed men stopped in the middle of looting the vehicle to look up at us.

One of them raised a sidearm but Eamon and I responded almost simultaneously, rounds from our rifles dropping the bandit before he could get off a shot. The others froze, one holding up his hands and stepping back behind what were now clearly hostages. He pulled aside scarf to reveal a heavily stubbled face and a slight smile.

"Cops? There aren't any cops left. I'm sure we can work something out here. These folks have plenty," he shouted up the hill in our direction.

Silverstein and Taylor slid down the hill coming to rest beside Eamon, holding up their hands.

"Look, fellah, I can tell you with no doubt in my mind this police officer isn't going to let you split the spoils and walk off. I'd put your weapons down and just walk away," Silverstein pleaded.

"No way am I letting these guys walk. They are criminals," Eamon growled.

"Wait, they might just be hungry and desperate people trying to survive," Taylor said tugging on Eamon's arm.

One of the highwaymen reached down and grabbed up a young girl pressing a knife to her neck. He looked up at us menacingly, his blade drawing a small amount of blood.

"No! Don't do that!" Silverstein cried out, eyes wide.

It was too late. Eamon roared so loud it shook the snow from the trees startling everyone on the scene. Letting his rifle drop on its strap, he charged down the hill on all fours toward the nearest highwayman. I snapped off a round at the guy with the knife, dropping him as I tried to get a bead on the others. Eamon was throwing up so much snow in his wake that I could barely see.

Eamon charged into the first guy hitting him so hard he cleared the thirty foot tall tree line, coming to rest some distance away, probably not all in one piece. The second highwayman got off a shot as Silverstein pulled Taylor to the ground for cover. They were firing handguns high and wild trying to hit Eamon. One stepped out from the crowd trying to get distance. I put a bullet in his ear as he raised his weapon to fire.

When the smoke cleared, Eamon was on the far side of the clearing having leapt over the hostages. He growled angrily, his breath escaping from between clenched teeth in long white plumes. A gigantic paw rested on the chest of the man that had been doing the talking before. He pressed in with his immense weight as the man struggled to breathe.

"Eamon! Stop! Stop!" Silverstein cried out, running down into the clearing.

Checking to make sure the hostages were okay, Taylor and I followed Silverstein over to where Eamon had the man pinned. Taylor put her hands on the huge Metasapient's arm and pleaded with him to let the man live.

"The girl's okay. She's just got a scratch. Please, you don't have to do this."

"He would have killed these people, or left them to freeze, starve, or worse. He's scum. Not worth protecting, and if it's like you've told me... there is no jail to put him in anymore," Eamon snarled, turning his broad head as to better meet Taylor's gaze.

"Should only the strong decide who lives and who dies? Is this how you want the world to be? What if everything is back to normal in a week?" Taylor said, hanging off Eamon's arm with all her weight.

Eamon's huge face softened slightly. "No, you're right. Unfortunately only the law can do that. I don't care what's happened to the rest of civilization, I'm still a cop. Always will be," Eamon replied, somewhat calmer.

For my own part, I was fine with Eamon ending the fool for what he'd done. That's not how it played out though. He slowly backed his paw off allowing the man to breathe then rose pulling out a pair of restraints with one smooth and practiced motion as if he'd done it ten thousand times.

"Maybe you didn't hear me before. I said, Armed Nordic Enforcement, cease and desist, you are under arrest."

CHAPTER 3

Ezra's War Journal, Part 5

Silverstein went around and freed the hostages. The highwaymen had employed zip ties and twine to bind their hands, which seemed to indicate some premeditation in their actions. Eamon was off seeing if the one he'd batted out into the trees was still alive.

"Thank you for your help," the eldest of the men said with a thick Scandinavian accent, rubbing the circulation back into his wrists.

"I hope Eamon didn't frighten you too much," Silverstein said. "From what he told us before, he's got nothing but hatred for people who take and harm hostages."

"Metasapients are an unpredictable lot to be sure. My name is Rupert Harjanne, I'm a doctor from Helsinki. This is my sister Marja and her husband Ahti Polvinen. We fled the chaos in Helsinki to try and find an outlying area off grid," the elderly man said, shaking Silverstein's hand.

"This your Snowcat?" Taylor asked, gazing covetously at the warm interior of the vehicle.

"Yes, I bought it so I could reach patients that lived in outlying areas during the winter. Would you like to warm yourself inside?" Dr. Harjanne offered.

Taylor bounded over to the Snowcat with Marja and the children, and waited patiently in line to enter. Ahti and Dr. Harjanne stood outside with Silverstein and me keeping watch over the highwayman that lay handcuffed in the snow at our feet. Ahti gazed at me for several moments before he finally spoke.

"I had a rifle like that when I was in the military. Are you a soldier?" he asked, gesturing to my rifle.

"For my tribe, yes," I said looking up at him.

"Ah! I thought you were a child at first," Ahti said, blushing.

"Ezra here is a pygmy Drone, his tribe is back in Port Montaigne in North America," Silverstein explained.

"You look very ill, Mr. Ezra," Dr. Harjanne said placing his hand on my forehead.

"Silverstein, I thought Drones just lived underground and turned wrenches and fixed leaks in the bigger cities. This one says he's a fighter of some sort?" Ahti said, the tone of his voice a little harder than before.

"Ezra is a Type One, a tailored life form designed for hazardous environment and EVA combat," Silverstein replied.

"You keep dangerous company with you, Mr. Silverstein," Ahti said meeting Dr. Harjanne's gaze.

Silverstein looked puzzled for a moment then smiled broadly.

"Don't worry, we aren't going to ask for a ride. If you follow the trail left behind by Eamon you'll find the cabin we were staying in. It has some food and enough chopped wood to last for quite a while. We're going toward the chaos you fled," Silverstein remarked with a slight sneer.

Ahti and Dr. Harjanne seemed relieved at the news.

"Here," I said as I handed Ahti my rifle.

"Won't you need this?" Ahti said, totally taken off guard by my gesture.

"I've another in the sled we brought, and a good rifle in the hands of someone who knew how to use it might have helped prevent what happened here," I said leaning heavily on Silverstein.

"Ahti, fetch my bag," Dr. Harjanne said kneeling down beside me.

The doctor listened to my hearts, looked in my eyes, ears, and throat. He looked grave before rising to his feet. Silverstein looked up at Taylor who was gazing down at us, forlorn, from the Snowcat window, her breath intermittently fogging the glass.

"I can't see that there is anything wrong with him that would afflict a human in this way. All three of his hearts are working overtime to keep him alive. Ezra, you probably exerted yourself way too much in the exchange with these thugs," Dr. Harjanne explained.

"Have you ever seen anything like this?" Silverstein inquired.

"Sort of. I've seen it in the elderly when they've been just deprived of a spouse they'd spent years with, before the sorrow killed him. Extremely rare that people form those sorts of attachments," Dr. Harjanne replied thoughtfully.

Feeling very tired, I sat down in the snow and looked over at the highwayman lying face down in the snow. He struggled to turn over and meet my gaze.

"Sounds pretty grim, you pint-sized freak, but no less than you deserve for shooting my friends," he rasped. He spat at me as far as he could.

Silverstein came unhinged, a strange fury overcoming him. He kicked the thug over onto his back and got one or two good shots in on his face before Dr. Harjanne and Ahti were able to pull him off. It was rare to see Silverstein angry, which is why I mention this at all.

Silverstein wiped his sleeve across his mouth and turned purposefully in my direction. He picked me up out of the snow and carried me back over to the Snowcat. Taylor made room for me on the bench seat beside her, and Silverstein set me down to head back out and talk to Eamon who had just returned.

"Is your daddy angry?" one of the children asked me.

"Yeah, Dad's mad," I replied, petting Taylor's fuzzy-snuzzy coat.

Taylor looked down at me and smiled.

"Do I need to make you one of these? You do look kind of cold," Taylor said, trying to hide her concern for me.

"It'd be terrible camouflage in a tactical situation, and it would result in the needless destruction of even more stuffed animals. Yeah, I think I need one," I replied, trying my best to take mind off my situation.

"This thing is pretty big, bet a dozen people could ride in it," Taylor said turning to Marja.

"My brother bought the largest one he could so it would serve as a mobile clinic. After he retired, he converted it to carry us all up into the hills during the tourist season. It's at least thirty years old, which is why it still works," Marja said, her voice trailing off.

"Are there a great many other vehicles that don't work?" Taylor asked.

"Anything marketed in the last twenty-five years that used the global grid for navigation, payment arrangement tracking, and similar was defunded and placed in lock down for repossession," Marja replied.

"Wow, a lot of people got behind on their bills," Taylor remarked.

"If you were able to ask the CGG AI, no one has the money to do so. It shut everything down, even outside of protocol. It locked down every hospital and defunded commercial transports and airlines while they were still in the air," Marja whispered, trying to avoid frightening the children further.

"What happened to the people on the airlines?" Taylor asked.

"They died," I said as quietly as I could.

Taylor looked deeply distressed. It was the first news she'd heard of the people she had been trying to save back at the server farm. When Silverstein and I pulled her from the terminal, saving her life, we knew there would be a terrible price that others would have to pay. Being a little jaded toward humans, I hadn't considered my own burden, let alone what Taylor would feel in the aftermath.

She wept bitterly. Marja tried to console her, and she couldn't have known what she was saying with what she said next.

"Please don't cry, none of this is your fault," Marja said putting a hand on Taylor's shoulder.

This only made her cry harder like I'd never seen. It was as if she could feel the weight of every death, her own highly advanced nature enabling her to literally calculate the likely number of maimed, wounded, and dead as a result of her being denied the opportunity to sacrifice herself for them. I felt awful for her, but if I had to do it over again, I'd rather have my friend than a few hundred million lousy humans, especially within the context of that moment.

I closed my eyes and resumed stroking the soft exterior of Taylor's multi-colored coat of fuzziness. Strange, in those near death circumstances the very small things we cling to for comfort. In that moment, I felt as apathetic as I did selfish. I wished it had occurred to me at the time how my own very jaded worldview had probably already changed the world.

Silverstein opened the compartment after a few moments, his face drooping at the sight of Taylor being so upset. He didn't need to ask what was wrong. He could guess by the bewildered looks on everyone's face but mine.

"We need to get going if we're going to find shelter before it gets dark," Silverstein said, directing his words more to me than to Taylor.

Taylor did her best to dry her eyes and helped me to my feet. We made our way off the Snowcat to where Eamon stood looming over the thug on the ground. Silverstein repacked the sled so I could sit in it while we traveled and made sure Taylor hadn't left her scarf in the Snowcat.

"It's in my pocket," she said, pulling it out and wrapping it about her neck.

"I didn't even know that thing had pockets," Silverstein said, smiling weakly.

"Of course it does," Taylor said pulling her handmade garment tightly around herself.

Taylor's hair slowly turned the color of the snow, a stark white as her skin became very pale and her eyes even darker brown. Her unconscious control of the tiny machines that made up her body was always startling, but it rarely betrayed her thoughts or her mood. More often, it signaled a fundamental change that had taken place, either by the trauma of what she endured, or the happiness from the things she enjoyed.

I was thankful that I was not so transparent.

Eamon shoved his prisoner along every once in a while, taking the lead while Silverstein pulled the sled and walked beside Taylor. I spent the time before it got dark doing my best to make my second rifle serviceable and pondering my own mortality. I didn't want to die, but if I did during the commission of what we'd done and seen, I was strangely at peace with the notion.

I wouldn't take my words and assume that all tailored life forms created to serve humans are as settled about death or the prospect thereof. We all have the same desire to live and survive. I think it was then I stopped to ponder all that had happened and the very real possibility that my own tribe, back beneath Port Montaigne, was in very real danger. I harbored that anxiety every day we spent traveling to Helsinki.

Images of people flooding the tunnels, hungry for any food they could find, or for warmth, or shelter, filled my mind. I could imagine my own people's desperate struggle to retain their comfortable home as humans sought any respite from the ensuing chaos above. I feared for them, and for all who lived off the grid. In having sought to be separate from those who relied on the CGG AI, they would be the first targets of those who had been betrayed by the same.

My own fears would be more fully realized the closer we got to Helsinki. In the three days previous to arriving at the city limits, we came across more than a few frozen bodies. Some had been the victims of violence, their naked bodies obviously looted for their possessions and their warm clothing. Others may have been the offenders, having lost their way in a white out and frozen to death before they could find suitable shelter.

Our own plight would have been no different without Eamon to show us the caves and hiding places in the wild that allowed us to at least take a few hours respite from the cold, or at least the wind. Along the way, Eamon did his best to obscure the tracks left by the Snowcat, his apprehension growing with each step.

Smoke rose from somewhere within the snow covered buildings of Helsinki that lined the horizon as we made our way along the main road. We decided to keep our distance from the road after finding an archaic automobile, riddled with gunfire, the occupants left to bleed to death in the cold. The trunk had been pried open, the theft of the contents being the motive for the attack.

A day later, we walked into Helsinki via an empty ditch normally reserved for excess run off from rain. We reached the city proper and ascended to the street level to find that the chaos had been mostly covered over by fresh snow. A few fires still smoldered, but the streets were mostly empty, at least as far as we could see.

"Death," Eamon said, sniffing the air.

Silverstein looked around puzzled for a moment as Eamon approached what appeared to be a pile of snow at the roadside. He brushed the snow away to reveal a frost covered man wearing a light coat and a hat. He looked to have fallen asleep there, his eyes still closed, when the cold took him. Taylor averted her gaze and walked around behind Silverstein to look in the opposite direction.

"Does Helsinki have places of shelter or private residences that are off the grid? Places where people could go?" Silverstein asked.

"Yes, but not that would support such a large displaced population. Then there are all the people that are probably trapped inside the buildings, having ignored the eviction protocols," Eamon said, trying to look through a tinted window. "They'll run out of water or food pretty quickly if they haven't already."

"We could break them out," Taylor said as she picked up a rock.

"Most of the buildings in central Helsinki were designed to resist terrorist attacks. If the shutdown occurred outside of protocols, which sounds likely, even pulling a fire release lever on a door or window wouldn't get you out," mused Eamon.

"Doubly the case when the buildings lose power," Silverstein observed.

"If no one can get into work or start up their work vehicle at Fortum Regional Power, that won't take too long. Especially with the snow we've been getting," Eamon added.

"It seems absolutely insane that these buildings would be that secure. There has to be a way to get into them, maybe from below?" Silverstein remarked, his irritation at the situation becoming more evident.

"Remember history? The old railroad barons, building the lines by the mile, and taking the government for a ride beyond the roundabout rail route? A lot of these buildings were built beyond code and far too quickly to not only meet compliance but to qualify for other incentives," Eamon said pulling out his satellite mobile.

"What if the government contracts to build all these buildings was part of the conspiracy behind the shut down?" Taylor asked. "It's something we've already considered to some degree. I'm starting to think it might be a trail of breadcrumbs leading to the bigger picture we can't see yet."

Silverstein was struck dumb for a moment, then looked to Eamon.

"What are you guys going on about? This is probably just a computer glitch or something," Eamon said, checking his mobile.

"You should let him go. He doesn't need to hear this and there's no jail, yeah?" Silverstein said pointing to the bandit Eamon had in custody.

Eamon seemed to resist the notion at first, but took the handcuffs off the bandit and sent him running. We watched him jog toward the highway for a minute or two before turning back toward our destination. Taylor eventually broke the awkward silence.

"It isn't a glitch," Taylor stated sadly, once the bandit was well out of earshot.

As we walked, she related to Eamon the whole story. She told him about Vance Uroboros, the Shut Down conspiracy, about Dr. Madmar and the server farm. She told him about her own attempts to foment the chaos we were walking through and why there were thousands of dead laying in the streets of Helsinki and probably every other major metropolitan city in the world.

"That means this thing is global!" Eamon exclaimed. "I didn't know you were mixed up in all this."

"Yeah, but you don't need to be. This isn't your problem, and once we figure out how to get out of here, it'll be our problem alone. Our burden," Silverstein replied.

"Are you really a terrestrial AI?" Eamon asked, while looking at Taylor.

"Yes," Taylor replied.

"I've never even heard of such a thing, but I suppose if they've got tailored life forms like myself, why not?" Eamon remarked. "If we find a building with power, do think you can open it?"

"I don't know. Possibly, we need to try to find a way to help Ezra first," Taylor said, putting her hand on my shoulder.

"Agreed," Eamon replied, clumsily tapping the touch screen on his mobile. "I'm going to have my fellow officers meet us at the hospital. Hopefully there are still satellites in orbit."

By that point, I'd started to feel more than ill. I felt something reaching out to me from the beyond. I feared that if I fell asleep I wouldn't wake up. It had grown difficult to breathe and I spent most of my time just trying to sit upright in the sled as Silverstein pulled it along the empty urban streets of Helsinki.

Taylor walked along beside me, babbling on about how she wished the shopping structures weren't locked down and what a nice thing it would be to have a hot cocoa. She was doing her best to cheer me up, even though I could sense she carried her own profound sorrow. I was the lucky one in that I had no idea why this depression was killing me. I bore no grudge against the terrible loneliness that had for days now began to strangle the life out of me.

With some frequency, Silverstein would stub his toe while treading through the snow behind Eamon. He declined to look down and see what it was, and I couldn't help but envision what lay beneath the snow and how terrible the spring thaw would be. The personal epiphany I'd felt back in the woods seemed so far away now. I couldn't help but mourn the passing of those moments, never to be experienced again.

At last, we reached what appeared to be a hospital. It was huge, and heavily fortified with a bomb resistant exterior composed of steel, concrete, and ballistic glass. Inside, people could be dimly seen but their faces were obscured by the tinted glass all around the ground floor. Eamon walked up to the entrance where there appeared to be several failed attempts to gain access. Someone had even swung a parking meter at the front glass, marring it slightly.

"I was only able to raise one other officer on the old auxiliary public. Should be here after a bit," Eamon said, pressing one of his great paws on the door.

People gathered on the inside near the door, probably hoping we were the aid they'd waited days for. Taylor lifted the cover on the emergency access pad. Someone had already undone the screws and the glass front of the access pad dropped out and hung by a few wires. Grasping the glass cover carefully, Taylor pressed it back into place and closed her eyes.

The pad lit up, without her even attempting a code. The buttons began to blink furiously as she attempted to isolate the access code. Eamon could only stand there and marvel at her ability to manipulate a device remotely with her thoughts.

"It won't accept any established user access codes," Taylor stated, her eyes remaining closed.

"Makes sense if the whole building has been toggled over to be repossessed," Silverstein remarked, turning a worried gaze toward me.

Taylor pulled out her own mobile and let her fingers glide across the touch screen for several moments. She looked up and down the road, her eyes coming to rest on a large commercial ground transport that had locked down in mid-delivery of its goods.

"I'm not carrying enough wattage to brute force a system locked down by the CGG AI. I need a large battery or two to draw from." Taylor's voice was calm.

I stood as best as I could and walked over to one of the commercial ground transports languishing beneath a layer of snow. The driver had been trapped inside, and scuff marks marred the interior of the driver's side window. The huge vehicle designed to repel hijackers and pirates in more dangerous countries turned into tombs in this somewhat safer country in the absence of the CGG AI's blessing.

Eamon grabbed the front of the grill and pulled with all his might until the hood latch could be seen. I threaded my slender hand in and unhooked it, allowing the hood to slowly ascend, pushing snow back to the windshield and onto the ground at our feet. He held me up so I could use my clawed hands to unhook wires and contact strips so we could get at the battery. Once it was free, Eamon lifted the large black block out of the vehicle's engine compartment.

We trotted back over and set the battery down in front of Taylor triumphantly. I had no idea how she intended to make use of the battery until I saw the interior of her multicolored coat drawn back. It had a steel mesh woven into the inside and several electrical leads she could use to garner contact with a power source and her own skin.

"Won't the stuffed animal skins melt from the heat?" Silverstein asked, somewhat stunned at the contraption.

"My own clothes would burn sooner," Taylor said smiling. "They started making stuffed animals heat resistant, nearly fire proof, about fifty years ago."

"Ah, that'd be why. I read one of those war correspondence articles on my phone last year, and it had pictures. In the Chinese civil war ten years ago, it seemed like whenever they would post pictures of a destroyed village or town, there would be stuffed animals that survived, laying in the wreckage," Eamon said.

"If only a child's joy could persist the calamity likely to follow," Silverstein added.

We all averted our eyes and turned our backs to Taylor creating a makeshift dressing room. There was probably no one to watch, but it at least shielded her from the wind as she slipped out of her clothes and back into her multicolored fuzzy-snuzzy coat. Draping the lip of the coat over the leads on the battery she immediately began to pull current from it.

Her hair and eyes began to glow brightly with an eerie luminescence, motes and tiny sparks of electricity leapt from her fingertips. She brought her hand within an inch of the control panel on the building making every button glow brightly as she began attempting to force the door controls to respond. I can only guess at what she was doing, but she gave off considerable and, considering the circumstances, welcome heat.

The doors shuddered as if she'd reached through and grabbed the program that controlled them by the neck. Moments later they slowly dithered back and forth parting only an inch or two. Taylor closed her eyes, seeming to really concentrate until the door obeyed, sliding to one side and locking into place, the small thin indicator light above them turning from red to green.

A cheer went up from inside and Taylor breathed a sigh of relief, white smoke escaping from her nose and mouth. Silverstein rushed to catch her as she stumbled and fell. He quickly pulled her coat off the battery and looked into her eyes. I staggered over as best as I could as Eamon stood between us and the crowd that ran cheering out into the street.

"Are you okay?" Silverstein asked her.

"Did I do it?"

Silverstein and I nodded as he held her up to see all the people able to finally go outside and breathe fresh air after days of being trapped inside. Some looked a little worse for wear, but they all had expressions of supreme relief, if not joy. I could see a modicum of the sadness Taylor had been feeling drift away with the steam coming off of her as she melted the snow around her. It almost looked like she was making a snow angel as she used the snow to dissipate the heat she built up carrying a higher than normal amount of wattage for the task.

The people in the hospital wouldn't have disputed my observation as they began battering Eamon with questions.

"Please stay near the hospital and don't go wandering off. This is probably the only shelter for miles now that people can get in and out of. Depending on how Miss Taylor feels, we might open more buildings. Please remain calm and orderly, thank you," Eamon said.

I sat down, the whole ordeal had exhausted me. I was relieved that Taylor hadn't hurt herself. After seeing her almost die in the server farm, I felt highly protective of her, something that seemed to bolster me in the midst of my loneliness. My respite was not to last as Eamon picked me up and set me on the edge of his arm as we walked into the hospital.

"You, are you a doctor?" Eamon bellowed, pointing at a man in a white coat.

"Yes, I am. Thank you for getting us out of here. We were starting to run out of food," the man said.

"I'm afraid that danger hasn't been averted. We'll need to get access to a warehouse, but I think that'll be possible after our, um... forcible entry agent has a chance to catch her breath," Eamon said after a moment to think.

The man's face went limp for a moment.

"Please, look at my friend here. He's sick," Eamon said gesturing to me.

"Hi, I'm Ezra," I said meekly.

"I'm Dr. Jeffrey Labs. Let's see if we can't find a room that still has power."

Dr. Labs was a younger human, maybe in his mid-thirties. He sported a beard I was certain he grew to give himself the appearance of wisdom as he would have seemed painfully young for a doctor otherwise. In spite of that fact, he seemed highly skilled, something the community would probably need if it were to survive the coming weeks.

The doctor did much of the same the other doctor did but took a scan of my body because he had the proper equipment. Using the emergency power still active in the examination room, he put the scans up on a display and pushed his glasses further up on his nose. Eamon peered in from the observation window, too large to fit in the room with us.

"Drone physiology isn't that far removed from humans, as we were the basis for your tailored genetic code. You have several special organs that were grown to help you adapt to hostile environments, see in low light conditions, hold your breath longer, withstand pressure, and so forth," Dr. Labs explained.

"How do you know all this? It's not exactly standard knowledge from what I understand," I said, somewhat suspicious of him.

"I served in the Orbital Navy during the colony incident on Mars. I treated a lot of Type One Drones like you. I've never seen a pygmy before, though. You aren't that different from your larger counterparts, but because of your increased physical strength, you don't have the same tolerance to hunger and thirst the larger Drones do. That level of physical strength requires more food and water than the norm. How long have you been combat active, and have you been eating enough?" Dr. Labs said pricking me with a child's sized needle for an analysis of my blood.

Silverstein and Taylor came into the room, laughing as if they'd just heard a joke. Taylor's hair was back to cool greens and blues, and she seemed like her old self. I looked up at them mournfully, feeling somewhat foolish.

"What's wrong with Ezra?" Taylor asked the doctor, the mirth quickly draining from her voice.

"He has a form of diabetes, not dissimilar from the sort that afflict humans," Dr. Labs replied. "He needs to eat relative to what a normal human does or his blood sugar crashes and he gets like this. Because of his increased regenerative abilities, it would take a really long time for this to kill him, but it's easily prevented by having 1-2 meals a day." The doctor handed Taylor a print out from his handheld.

"We were pretty sure this had something to do with a mystic connection to his tribe and that he needed to find Drones to hang out with," Silverstein said smiling, obviously relieved.

"No. If he were a Metasapient of a type that shared a hive mind or psychic link, then something like that might be the case. As far as I'm aware, there are no psychic Drone colonies," Dr. Labs said winking at me.

Taylor looked as though she were going to say something, but thought better of it as several people had gathered outside to get a look at me. Eamon, satisfied I was being helped, turned and dispersed them with a growl.

Dr. Labs put me on an intravenous drip and gave me a slightly wilted apple from the hospital cafeteria. In thirty minutes or so, I felt like myself again, and in contrast, better than I had felt in days. The doctor then removed the drip, swabbed the wound the IV left behind, and waited for a moment as my flesh knitted back together. He offered me a lollipop.

"Put that in your pocket, just in case you need a little boost or have to skip a meal for some reason. I don't recommend that you regularly have sugar straight up like this but it'll work in a pinch," he said.

I didn't protest. I have a deep and abiding love of root beer flavored candy.

CHAPTER 4

HELSINKI, FINLAND

January 21st, 2200

Ezra's War Journal, Part 6

    The day following the liberation of Helsinki General consisted of wandering about looking for a warehouse and using the old auxiliary public to try and notify people still looking for shelter that there was some to be had and where. When we finally found a warehouse that might have what we were looking for, it was unpowered and lacked door controls on site. This didn't deter us. Eamon and I took turns through the early morning hours battering one of the overhead doors down with a sledge hammer.

    I worried about the noise we were making, but worried more about my stomach going without food. When we'd made enough of a gap for me to slip through, I went inside and began slipping food out to many waiting and hungry hands. The warehouse wasn't particularly full, but the food was still good and well packaged, a lucky find that was not to be repeated any time soon.

    "This is just a distribution warehouse. The larger ones will have doors we can't break down," Eamon said stuffing his pockets.

    Making her way through the crowd, I could see a Canine Metasapient wearing the same sort of tactical gear as Eamon. She was tall with pristine white fur and unnervingly blue eyes. There were flecks of blood across her face and shoulders. She smelled of death and gunpowder. Eamon saw her too and called out to her.

"Abbey, are you alright?" Eamon bellowed as he made a path to her out in the crowd.

"Eamon! Hello," she responded.

Taylor and I wandered along behind Eamon while Silverstein continued to hand out food to the crowd. There was something odd about this particular law dog. I couldn't put my finger on it at first. It wasn't until I got close that I realized she wasn't a Type Two Metasapient. It was far more likely she was like myself, a Type One, similarly trained. A tailored life form with only two functions, survive and kill the enemy.

She regarded me in much the same way that I did her, with caution. I don't know how we were able to recognize each other to this day. We just sort of knew.

"Eamon, where is the rest of our patrol division?" Abbey asked.

"You are the only one I've been able to contact. The others are probably still on patrol in outlying areas. They might not even know what has transpired yet. I wouldn't have if it weren't for these folks," Eamon explained, as he gestured to Taylor and me.

"Patrolling in outlying areas, or dead," Abbey said, as if to finish what Eamon had avoided to say.

"What makes you think that?" Taylor said, interjecting.

"You the one that opened the hospital?" Abbey replied, momentarily ignoring the question.

"Yes."

"There are humans that believe Metasapients are abominations, and they form secret organization and cults to that end. I wouldn't be surprised if they used the current lawlessness to try to kill us," Abbey explained.

Taylor and I left Abbey and Eamon alone to talk after that, heading back over to where Silverstein was standing. He handed off the last of the food and clapped invisible dust from his hands, garnering some satisfaction at having helped the hungry crowd. I wondered about this human practice, but declined to ask about it.

"Looks like we've got another Metasapient member of law enforcement as an ally. Where are the human cops?" Silverstein asked.

"They wouldn't have the same compulsion to serve as Metasapients would, having had it hard coded into their DNA," I responded, without really understanding the intent behind Silverstein's question.

Silverstein smiled weakly.

"I don't like her. There's something scary about her," Taylor said, looking over her shoulder at Abbey.

"What do you mean?" Silverstein inquired.

"She's not a law enforcement model Metasapient. She's a Type One like me," I reported calmly.

"A soldier? I didn't think they made Type One Canine Metasapients," Taylor replied.

"She's the only one I've ever seen," I said, mirroring Taylor's concern.

"What's the big deal? She's a soldier like you, right?" Silverstein asked.

I stopped to consider my next words carefully.

"She's not supposed to exist. I can only think of a couple of reasons for her being here. She was a one-time test to see if a stable Type One Canine could be created and trained..."

"Or?" Taylor asked.

"She can hear us," I said, using my peripheral vision to gauge her body language.

Abbey looked visibly upset and self-conscious, somewhat dispelling my suspicion that she had been manufactured by Dr. Madmar and planted in the area to watch over his operation. I didn't have the degree of hearing she did, but I could see her almost tearfully trying to explain something to Eamon before he came back over to us.

Eamon nodded. She was probably telling him what I'd already figured out, that she wasn't what she seemed to be. Eamon didn't care and patted her on the shoulder reassuringly. I felt terrible for even bringing the matter to anyone's attention.

"Hi, I'm Abbey," she said, shaking Silverstein's hand, then Taylor's, and then mine.

The palm of her hand felt leathery and tough across my palm and soft across the back as my fingers circled around her hand. She had a gentle, almost ingratiating handshake.

"Silverstein."

"I'm Taylor," Taylor said, employing her warmest smile.

I introduced myself, but couldn't meet her gaze.

"When I first moved here, I was assigned to guard a man who worked on an important project for the CGG. After he died, I felt pretty lost until Eamon convinced me to join Nordic Enforcement," Abbey explained.

"MDC Project?" I inquired.

"Yes," Abbey said, avoiding my gaze.

"You're old like me then," I surmised.

Abbey clenched her teeth and nodded.

"I'm pretty old, almost twenty-two," Eamon interjected trying to lighten the mood.

Silverstein looked as though he were going to say something but I shushed him with a glance and a slight shake of the head. Taylor caught it too and just nodded to Eamon and smiled. Abbey turned her gaze to the rapidly dispersing crowd and cleared her throat before wandering off to join them.

"Looks like people are heading back to the hospital for the night. Meet you guys there?" Eamon asked.

"Yeah, we'll be there in a bit," Silverstein said with an easy smile.

We started back after they'd gone ahead a ways and it was just Silverstein, Taylor, and I walking together somewhere behind the pack.

"Think she can hear us?" Taylor asked.

"Yeah, she's an unmitigated Metasapient. She can probably hear a flea scream as it falls off a dog's back a mile away," I replied.

"I'm an amnesiac, remember? I don't know what any of this means," Silverstein said half-joking.

"The original MDC Project was started almost ninety years ago. It produced a handful of Metasapients and Drones based on the original genetic tailoring and designs. They were quickly feared for their abilities and the project was almost shut down for being too successful," I explained.

"What happened? Taylor asked, walking a little slower.

"Remember the guy claiming to be Dr. Helmet? What if he wasn't dead, and that really was him? What if Madmar lied and Matthias was wrong?" I posited.

"It sounds like I cloned myself. What if Madmar and Helmet have done the same thing?" Silverstein replied.

"You're almost ninety. Why is she so worried about Eamon or the others knowing how old you guys are?" Taylor replied.

"Unless they're psychic, Drones and Metasapients don't live much past fifty, let alone retain their physical prowess beyond that age. We're not certain how old the original unmitigated Drones and Metasapients can get, and we don't like to advertise that we even exist," I replied, trying not to be curt.

"Wow, good to know in the future for avoiding awkward conversations with you and Abbey," Silverstein replied, obviously unsatisfied with my answer.

"The original Type One Drones were supposed to be protectors, to keep humanity safe, or to persist in the aftermath if the human race couldn't survive some calamity. This assumes the man calling himself Dr. Helmet was the real deal. I only just barely remember my training when I went through manufacturing," I replied, wringing my hands anxiously.

"How does meeting Abbey change or affirm any of that?" Silverstein questioned.

"She stayed when so many others humans and Metasapients fled to save themselves. The moment I saw her, I knew she was different. She's got the stink of death on her, but also a profound sadness. She's had to kill a human or two recently, but I'll bet it was because she was between them and someone helpless that needed to be defended," I replied with certitude.

"How can you know all that by just seeing and talking to her for a few minutes?" Taylor said with a slight giggle.

"It's in everything she does; her body language, tone of voice, the way she regards humans with some sort of respect. These days, I feel nothing but a healthy disdain for them," I replied, somewhat ashamed.

"What are you talking about?" Silverstein said, almost demanding.

"Those guys back there that had Dr. Harjanne's family hostage. I shot them without hesitation or remorse. That doesn't seem right," I said, trying to sort out how I was really feeling.

"Sounds like you're feeling pretty bad about it now. Between them being assholes and Eamon going berserk, it's not like you had a choice," Silverstein observed.

He was right of course. I did feel pretty bad about it.

"What about the alien invasion the Drones were tailored to help repel? You think any of that was real?" Taylor asked.

"Gods, I don't know," I said picking up the pace a little.

We walked in the snow for an hour, behind the shuffle of the rest of the group. I was relieved to see the hospital rise in the distance, even if the whole structure was almost entirely dark. I was looking forward to being able to sleep and share the night watch with others in shifts. I was really beginning to feel my age.

When we got inside, they moved a couple of heavy curtains in front of the door to help deter the cold. I found an old army jacket that someone had discarded behind the chairs in the waiting room and curled up on it, my rifle tucked in at my side. I must have slept all night because no one woke me for a shift to watch the door.

I rubbed my eyes and looked out into the waiting area. Abbey was standing in the foyer looking out the large windows into the snowy streets outside. Defused morning light filtered in giving the interior of the hospital some dim illumination to accompany the flickering emergency lighting. The law dog's ears twitched slightly before going calm again at intervals, detecting sound both faint and distant.

I rolled out of my nest and wandered over to where Abbey stood. She didn't break her vigil, continuing to look out into the streets. I turned and looked in the same direction she was and saw a bit of smoke rising in the distance, just beyond the skyline.

"Why didn't you wake me for a shift, I'd have watched for a few..."

"There was no point, I couldn't sleep," she whispered.

"Sorry about yesterday. I haven't even really told my friends about what precious little I remember about the MDC Project," I offered, still feeling a little embarrassed over the whole thing.

"All night, I've been hearing gunfire and screams. Other than the few peaceful folks we've been able to gather together here, the city and the out-lying areas are tearing itself apart. People are hungry, cold, and desperate as a consequence. They had been wandering away from the core part of the city, but the unrest seems to be drawing closer," Abbey said quietly, her cold blue eyes still fixated on the street outside.

"Gunfire?"

"Mostly small arms, but it sounds like there may be rogue military units and reserves operating out there for their own benefit. I have heard larger guns being employed," she said, unconsciously checking her own gear with a free hand.

"This open hospital door is like a metaphor for your whole life, isn't it?" I said, knowing something of how she felt.

"Indeed. The innocent people behind me are counting on me to keep them safe, and the desperate folks in front of me are already victims of their own humanity," Abbey said.

"Victims?" I asked, not understanding.

"They wouldn't have created me if they trusted themselves to keep each other safe. Humans needed a third party to act in their best inter-ests. It's simply their nature to kill, rape, and destroy one another," Abbey stated plainly.

"I'm somewhat relieved to hear you say that," I replied, after a moment of thought.

"Thought you were the only tailored life form that had become jaded after decades of watching humanity do everything it could to devour itself?"

"Truly."

Abbey smiled slightly, then immediately resumed her vigil.

"Probably better go find Eamon and your friends," Abbey whispered, pulling her shotgun tighter to her shoulder. "It sounds like someone has managed to get an old armored personnel carrier operational."

"You sure it's going to be a problem?"

"They are headed this way, using the armored vehicle to kill people and loot more lightly fortified buildings for what they need. It's only logi-cal to assume they'll come to the hospital eventually," Abbey replied.

I grabbed Abbey by the arm and turned her to face me. She looked down at me, visibly annoyed by me disturbing her concentration.

"Why are we waiting for them to come here? We should just go to them and put a stop to it before they ever get here," I suggested politely.

"They've got military grade weaponry and an armored transport, we should try to fight them from a fortified position, if it comes to that," she replied, jerking her arm from my grasp.

"You aren't thinking like a soldier," I said turning to go find Eamon.

I walked down the hallway into a longer hallway. Eamon sat at the far side. He was sleeping peacefully, propped up against a wall, his arm draped over an arm chair where Taylor was also fast asleep. Silverstein was sitting on the floor on the other side of the chair, his eyes scanning the screen on his mobile. Seeing me, he stood quietly as not to wake the others.

"Uh oh, you've got that look on your face," he said pocketing his mobile.

"Abbey can hear an armored transport off in the distance. It's carrying what are likely rogue soldiers who are looting and killing their way through the city. She thinks they'll eventually come here and try to get medical supplies," I reported.

"The vehicle has the guns or the horsepower to crack open buildings?" Silverstein inquired.

"Sounds like it, or they've got a Mechanic with them," I whispered.

"We've got to go find them. Try to stop them before they even get here," Silverstein said looking back at Taylor and Eamon.

"This is why we are friends," I replied.

"Huh, oh really?" Silverstein whispered with a smile.

"Abbey thinks we should try to mount a defense here."

"There are too many innocent people, healthy and sick in here. It's too risky," Silverstein said, shaking his head.

We both knew that Abbey could probably hear us talking if she wanted to, but I didn't care. In my opinion she was being foolish and a little bit cowardly, something I had hardly expected from her. We needed to stop the armored transport somehow before it even got there, and with Eamon, Taylor, Silverstein, and I working together it might just be possible.

After waking Eamon and Taylor, I explained to them the situation and put forward a plan of action. After everyone was clear on what to do, we gathered up what we thought we'd need and prepared to headed out. We walked to the entrance of the hospital where Abbey continued her watch of the street outside.

"You sure you won't come with us?" I asked.

"Someone should stay here. I'm sure these aren't the only looters and desperate folks out there," Silverstein offered, trying to broker a compromise.

"He's right, Ezra. Someone needs to hold the fort while we're gone," Taylor said.

I hesitantly agreed. I could tell this wasn't about having an ego or being right for Abbey. It was about doing what she felt was right regardless. Even if I didn't agree with her, I could respect her decision. That being said, it would have been really nice to have her with us for what happened next.

The four of us crept down alleys and through drainage canals until we could hear the sound of a huge engine propelling a tracked vehicle across the pavement nearby. Silverstein took out the expensive watch the doctor had loaned us and put on the nicest coat we could find. Taylor did much the same thing by putting on the richest clothes we'd been able to scrounge, and willing her hair to assume an appearance, I'm told, looked "fresh from the salon." I didn't like it.

We made our way the last few blocks until we came upon the large military transport. It had two anti-personnel turrets and sported an armored frame that was suspended several feet above the pavement, it's tracked wheel base like that of an army tank, but broader. I'd never seen one before, but they were supposed to be resistant to mines and attempts to hack their systems from the ground.

They'd used the winch on the front, probably intended to lay down temporary bridges, to pull the doors off of a convenience store. Most of them, still in their CGG military uniforms, were inside loading up a pair of shopping carts. They had their rifles casually slung over their shoulders as they moved goods from the store to the transport.

I watched as Silverstein and Taylor approached them, watching carefully for the signal.

"Lieutenant, we've got civvies out here," one of the soldiers said, calling up to the open hatch on the APC.

From my vantage point I could see that they'd already removed their name plates and anything that would identify them with a particular unit. They were equipped like an engineering group though, not infantry. Silverstein launched into his part, playing it admirably.

"I could hear you from some distance away, have you come to rescue us?" Silverstein said nervously.

What looked to be the person in charge dropped from the vehicle to the ground and walked over to where Silverstein, Taylor and two other soldiers stood. Taylor did her best to be friendly in a way I've heard human females can be. The behavior still baffles me.

"Sir, there's not likely to be any rescue. The CGG shut down went global a day ago," the "Lieutenant" said, obviously mocking Silverstein.

The other soldiers smiled in a way I didn't like. It was obvious they intended to survive whatever had happened by taking what they needed or wanted from others, by force. Eamon and I moved into our respective positions and prepared for the worst.

One of the soldiers pushed Silverstein down, then dropped the butt of his rifle hard to his midsection and grabbed Taylor by the arm. It had gotten ugly faster than we thought it would. We'd intended to try and lure them to a more enclosed location, away from their vehicle, with the promise of access to a vault in a building that was independently powered. Silverstein was to tell them he knew the access codes and that the contents would be worth their while, outlawed rejuvenation drugs were to be our ruse.

"Wait, I've something to bargain with," Silverstein pleaded, doing his best to stay in character.

"I agree," the Lieutenant replied, taking Taylor by the arm.

He dragged Taylor back toward the APC as the two other soldiers stepped in closer to Silverstein. What I saw through the scope of my rifle wasn't part of the plan by any stretch, but Taylor must have thought she knew what she was doing. She reached over and touched the APC and did something that should have been impossible. She used what I assumed was tele-mechanic force to cause it to stall and shut down, the engines and systems going quiet.

The men cried out, and the Lieutenant released his grasp and turned to look up at the vehicle. I could hear him barking orders, but he was cut short as Taylor grabbed his sidearm and discharged it into his midsection. I was a little shocked, but quickly snapped out of it. Eamon and I opened fire, single shot only, from our respective sniping positions. He was lurking behind a dumpster in the alley and didn't have the same field of fire I did from a ledge two stories up.

The idea was that he'd be able to fire on them if they went beneath the vehicle for cover and I'd be able to get at them if they scattered. We dropped two of them before the rest disarmed Taylor and pulled both her and Silverstein inside the convenience store. I tried to get another shot in to try to prevent the hostage situation, but it was too risky.

I knew I had to get in there somehow, and stop them from hurting my friends. I dropped from the ledge and crossed the street as Eamon moved to a position behind one of the APC's enormous tank treads. Eamon was huge, it would take him a moment to squeeze through the door into the interior. I would have to be the first one in to cover him.

The Lieutenant was still on the ground, bleeding heavily from the stomach and cursing. He dragged himself over to one of the soldiers we'd sniped and recovered a rifle trying his best to stay in cover. Eamon waved me off from trying to get a shot on him, pointing to the upper level of the convenience store. I could see movement from inside, then the windows slowly opening as someone turned the emergency escape cranks to allow egress.

They'd have a great shot at anyone who tried to enter the building from the front, and the rear access was probably armored like every other building in the downtown core. I slid along the ground through the snow and refuse as close as I could.

"We've got your friends. Don't know how you shut our rig down, but you'll be turning it back on if you ever want to see them alive," one of the soldiers called out from an upper window.

"Your boss is injured badly, he'll die without medical assistance. We've access to that sort of assistance, but there's nothing to be done as long as this standoff persists," Eamon shouted back.

One of the soldiers stepped out with Taylor as a shield. Eamon peaked out from his position and nodded to the soldier. He moved forward so that

Taylor was outside and he was still obscured by the building itself, at least from my vantage.

He ordered Taylor to go out and recover the injured lieutenant. She seemed to hesitate but she slowly moved out into the open. Kneeling down next to the injured soldier, she let her hand brush up against the APC. It suddenly started up again, the engine idling as it had before.

Before anyone could react, the access ladder retracted and the side hatch on the APC shut with a loud clank. It rumbled to life and began to slowly roll down the street, with Eamon keeping time with it, as to not lose his cover. The soldier holding Taylor hostage ran out into the street and reached down to pick up the Lieutenant in the confusion.

I watched carefully, waiting for an opportunity. Taylor stepped underneath the APC, and stepped back around the slow moving treads just out of reach. The soldier cursed and began pulling his fallen comrade back toward the building.

The APC made a lot of noise. It was all I could do to hope it would be enough to cover what I was about to do next. I squeezed off a round, felling the soldier, and began to run forward. The lieutenant dropped to the ground beside his fallen ally, trying to pick up a rifle but Eamon stepped in, crushing him underfoot.

I didn't break stride as I rounded the corner into the convenience store. Bags of snacks crunched under my feet as I plowed into three soldiers waiting just round the corner. I moved as quickly as I could, past the muzzles of their rifles and clawed at their legs and abdomens. They fell to the ground behind me, bloodied and turning their rifles to fire at me. Eamon squeezed through the door behind them and trampled them as he made his way toward the center of the store.

I knew I wouldn't be able to ascend the stairs in time to save Silverstein. Fortunately, Eamon had a way of giving us some more time. Stepping in behind me, he put his shoulder to one of the support pillars in the room, then clawed out the other. The false ceiling came down, and the floor above with it. Eamon stepped over me as an avalanche of building materials, filing cabinets, and people fell from the upper level.

Clawing his way upward, Eamon made a hole, tossing aside anything that got in his way, roaring as a real bear would, only much, much louder. If the soldiers weren't stunned from the fall, they would be by the sound.

I followed Eamon up and over the refuse that had fallen, dust and muzzle flare filling the air.

We moved out in opposite directions, staying low as our adversaries fired blind, our rifles down and claws out. They didn't have a chance. When the dust cleared, I found Silverstein lying face down, his hands over his head. He coughed and turned over to look up at me.

"Wow, that did not go as planned," Silverstein said, coughing, almost unable to breathe.

"Lucky for you, what they build on the inside of these armored facades isn't nearly as tough as what they build on the outside. Makes it easier to redecorate for new commercial tenants that come in to replace the old," Eamon replied, wiping the blood from his claws onto the tattered remnant of a plaid travel blanket.

We stumbled back outside to find the APC had stopped about a block up the street. Taylor was sitting in the snow up against the inside of one of the treads. She was very still, and my heart sank the closer we got.

Once we closed the gap, it was clear she'd caught a bullet in the exchange, her exquisite dress marred by blood right below the left collarbone. Silverstein stooped down and picked her up, trying to get some sort of response. There was none.

"Goddamn it, Ezra, how could this have happened?" Silverstein said angrily.

"I don't know! Everyone else was in the building, and any shot out the doorway would have hit me as I was going in," Eamon said, just as confused.

I turned and looked back down the street. We were just at the edge of the downtown core and there were several buildings only a block away that were archaic and probably off-grid. One, standing at the end of a t-intersection had a single window open, yellow curtains blowing in the wind. It wasn't the soldiers that had shot Taylor, it was someone else.

"There," I said pointing.

"We should get out of here before whoever it was decides to shoot at us," I said pushing Silverstein into an adjoining alley.

Eamon and I walked along behind Silverstein as we made our way back to the hospital as quickly as we could. The APC followed along behind us like a stray dog rolling at the same pace while keeping to the main streets that could support its girth. There was nothing we could do about it, and we were much relieved when it shut down just outside the hospital.

Silverstein rushed Taylor inside and into the only examination room that still had power. Dr. Labs came in and examined Taylor, his expression grim. She'd stopped breathing moments before we arrived and had lost a lot of blood in spite of our best efforts to keep pressure on the wound.

I had to wonder if someone such as her could really be killed, or if perhaps she'd been programed to cease functioning in the event that she sustained an injury that would kill a normal person. Maybe whoever created her had wanted her to live life as it was meant to be lived, with a sense of her own mortality. I hoped desperately that would not be the case.

Regardless, it was my intent to go out and find whoever had shot her and get revenge. I was no good to anyone waiting around in the hospital. I gave Eamon a nod, checked my rifle, and headed for the door. Abbey was still standing vigilantly at the front entrance.

"I'm sorry about what happened to your friend," Abbey said as I walked past.

"It didn't have to end up like this," I replied angrily.

"Going out to find the person responsible?" Abbey replied calmly.

I could only stand there and fume. I didn't know what to do next.

"Ezra, whoever it was, they're probably long gone," Abbey said as she faced me. "It could have been anyone, even a vengeful civilian. Those rogue soldiers had to make a few enemies as they rolled through the older parts of the city."

She was right of course. If there was anything I'd learned about humans since the shutdown it was that they would likely go one of two ways in the aftermath; barbarous desperation or something else entirely across the broad range of the human spectrum.

CHAPTER 5

Truman from Accounting

Phelps trudged along beside Walter, the three coats he was wearing barely staving off the cold of the Finnish winter. They'd been walking for almost three days and sleeping wherever they could find a modicum of shelter or warmth. Each step they took was following in the footsteps of a man who had promised them a return to modern luxury. This was a man who had just the day before flirted with their boss and taken a yogurt that did not belong to him from the fridge in the break room.

"Truman, is it much farther?" Walter whined, trying to rub the cold from his arms.

"Is not far now, you'll see," Truman replied.

"How are you not cold, Truman?" Phelps asked, looking at Truman's business casual.

"Sometimes, where I am from, it would get cold like this. You learn to block it out, let your body, how you say...acclimate," Truman replied jovially.

Walter looked over at Phelps with the same mournful eyes that he had every mile or so and shook his head. Phelps shot him an angry glare in response and walked faster to keep up with Truman. It was beginning to snow.

Truman was a big man, heavy from too many microwaved burritos but strong. He seemed to have no trouble making his way through the snow deeper into the woods. They'd been traveling north for hours and it would be dark soon. They'd crossed a major highway a ways back and were making their way into the dense timbers tourists would hike in during the summer.

"I wonder how the people trapped on the islands are doing, the last time I checked the auxiliary public network, the bridges had all been closed," Walter whispered to Phelps. "I'm sure there are no commercial boats or water transports running. How will people get out of there?"

Phelps just shook his head, trying to avoid the conversation.

"It is too bad Marjorie could not come, yes?" Truman said, trudging through the snow.

"Do your brother and sister really have a transport out here? We'll need to find shelter soon," Phelps replied.

"When I come here, it was with a forged identity and CV. I was supposed to infiltrate your debt collection bureau and find someone inside to help us steal money," Truman stated, matter of fact.

"What? What are you talking about?" Phelps replied.

"I am thief. My brother and sister and I were going to steal money, using your own computers. It wasn't our plan. A man came to us with idea. It was a good plan, until today," Truman added, somewhat disappointed, as if he'd lost a sock or spilled milk.

Phelps suddenly wished he'd listened to Walter and stayed with Abbey.

"Did you manage to steal any money?" Walter asked, trying to keep things friendly.

"No. During surveillance we watch your boss Marjorie. The plan was to turn her and use our combined access to steal money for FLF," Truman replied.

"Financial Liberation Front? They're terrorists!" Phelps exclaimed, somewhat shocked.

"Or rebels if you like. Anyway, we were doing our surveillance of your boss and do you know what? She sings in the shower. Now, she does not sing like what you would think. She sings as a beautiful song bird kept in a gilded cage. I fell in love with her voice," Truman continued, clasping his hands to his breast.

"You watched her shower?" Walter replied, somewhat in awe.

"No, no, we are not barbarians. Anyways, we only listen to her conversations, the things she did at home, that sort of thing. No eyes-on watching. I would never have taken away her dignity like that. Now, my cousin, he has other idea. He says we are going to take her after operation and sell her to a skin trafficker, a man who trades in people," Truman continued, regaining his previously jovial tone.

"No..." Phelps replied, looking around for a means of escape.

"You know what I did? I shoot him. My own cousin would sell someone with a voice like that, for only the chance to feel money in his pocket? I shoot him, and I spit on him," Truman said, spitting for emphasis.

"You... you're insane," Walter blurted.

Truman stopped and turned suddenly, sticking a handgun in Walter's already bruised ribs.

"Quiet, little man. I am telling story," Truman said, his mustache bristling with every word. "Anyway, the man who gave us job was not happy, saying that I compromise whole operation. He did not know we were all family. His plan to give each our own bit of the operation while keeping us in dark about the rest failed," Truman continued.

Phelps walked along, eyeing the handgun still dangling in Truman's hand. The man was easily twice his size and Walter was in his current state of health likely to be no help. He would have to wait and see how this played out.

"I did not care. All I really wanted was to be with Marjorie and to hear her sing. I do my best to woo her, but I am clumsy in these things. I did not take it personally, as she was a gifted flower. And me? I am only thief," Truman lamented.

"I'm sorry. I didn't know you felt that way, I'd have put in a good word," Phelps replied, feigning empathy as best he could.

"Is okay. I did not deserve such a woman, perhaps no man does." Truman waved his pistol as he talked. "I was like sailor listening to some far away melody, only to be dashed on the rocks. I had a recording of her singing, it was very nice. Still, I wish she could have come with me. I would, for her, done anything."

Walter looked ahead and could see a medium sized commercial transport painted orange, the color assigned to neutral operators, but just as often employed by thieves and mercenaries. The team he traveled with to South America used such a vehicle as cover for their activities. He could smell something cooking over a fire in the distance.

"That your brother and sister up ahead?" Phelps asked.

"As I was getting ready to leave town, do you know what happened?" Truman asked, the joviality to his voice draining away.

"No. What happened?" Phelps asked.

"I found her, like withered flower in the snow. She is laying in the street, discarded like trash. She was still alive when I asked who left her there. She gave me two names," Truman continued.

"Wait. Truman, there was nothing we could do," Phelps said stopping in his tracks.

Truman stopped and turned to face Phelps and Walter. He looked down at them with a face that betrayed intense sorrow. Phelps raised his hands and tried to think of something he could say to console Truman, but the words did not come.

"You two left her there. To die. Did you sit with her as I did? Did you beg her to sing and get nothing in response as she took her last breath? No, you were off trying to make yourselves as comfortable as you are now. You were thinking only of yourself. I am thief, but I still have a soul. I can love!" Truman stammered as tears began to streak down his face.

"Truman, I'm really sorry, I..." Walter began, feeling genuine remorse.

"I have killed men, and you may think I'm a monster. This, I accept. But, what you did on the street outside where you work shows that you are the real monsters. What will you do now? Alone in woods with no heated home, no machine to make you coffee, and no upper management people to tell you what to do? What do you do now, tiny men?!" Truman roared.

"I have money. I've been funneling it away secretly for two years. Get me a terminal, I'll put it into whatever account you like. Please, don't kill us," Phelps said, keeping his voice calm while raising his hands.

Truman turned the handgun on Phelps and fired two rounds into his chest at point-blank range. Phelps fell to the ground, blood rushing to the surface of his clothes as he coughed more up onto the snow beside him. He cried out in pain, and grasped at the snow in a vain attempt to crawl away. Walter froze, holding up his hands and closing his eyes.

"Yes, crawl like worm that you are. You can keep your money, all I ever wanted was Marjorie. To hear her sing. You cannot trade lives for a lifestyle and still be human!" Truman bellowed shooting Walter in the face.

Phelps turned and raised a bloody hand in a vain attempt to protect himself. Truman picked up Walter's still twitching corpse and placed it inside Phelp's coat beside him. Phelps looked up, choking on blood and unable to speak, his eyes wide with shock.

"I want you to die like she did. I am not monster, so I would not leave you with a dead child. Walter is next best thing, and I never liked him anyway. Talked too much. Now, do you know what I did after she died?" Truman said standing up, making sure Phelps was as comfortable as he could make him.

Phelps shook his head.

"I bury her with audio record of her singing. Was the only copy I had, but I could not bear to think of her without her voice, and I was not so selfish as to take from her. I wanted to take nothing from her, only give. Do you understand?" Truman explained.

Phelps nodded as best he could.

"Good. You will not get a burial by someone who love you. I do not know if they have wolves here, but if they do, they will be your pallbearers. Good day," Truman said, giving a slight wave as he turned and headed down the other side of the hill toward the clearing.

Phelps gurgled, trying to rise but fell back against the snow, the weight of Walter laying inside his long coat holding him down. He tried to push him off, but his chest burned like fire every time he tried. It was getting cold now, and the sun was going down.

Truman finished walking into the clearing where a group of heavily armed men and women awaited him. He hugged his brother Dragos and his sister Tullia as he stepped close to their cooking fire and grasped hands with several other men. Matthias watched from the hold where they had him chained with casual interest.

"Good to see you both," Truman said warming his hands by the fire.

"Everything okay? We heard shots," Dragos asked, sitting down next to larger younger brother.

"You look good, Dragos. Your hair is long, and you've put on the good kind of weight since I last see you," Truman replied leaning to one side on his brother.

Dragos had done two tours in South America for the cause in the last three years. He'd seen more bloodshed and war than soldiers working for the CGG twice his age. He'd grown hard from the experience, but nothing melted his icy heart like seeing the sorrow on his little brother's face.

"Tell Dragos, what is the matter?" Dragos inquired.

"Remember woman I told you about?" Truman asked taking a plate of food from Tullia.

"Yes-yes, do we go to get her now?" Dragos replied.

Truman shook his head mournfully as he took a bite of some bacon.

"She would not have you?" Tullia asked protectively.

"I will never really know. She got hurt, and the people that should have been her friends left her in the cold. I found her too late," Truman said, tears flowing freely.

"These 'friends', you found them?" Tullia asked angrily, kneeling down beside Truman.

"The shots you heard. I take care of it," Truman said patting his younger sister on the shoulder.

"Good. I would expect nothing less. You do always take care of things, brother," Dragos said filling Truman's steel cup with more coffee.

"Sister, I like your ship very much. How is your work doing salvage?" Truman asked, feeling a little bit better.

"Not exactly, and your English is getting better, Truman," Tullia said.

Dragos laughed a little bit.

"What? Tell me," Truman said smiling broadly.

"I did a job up north, in the Arctic. Man that hire you to do job, hire us to go there and check out an abandoned installation. It was full of valuable things, Metasapients, and a Mechanic marooned there after a fight with bug things," Tullia replied.

"Mechanic? This is good?" Truman replied.

"Not a regular mechanic. He is the psychic kind," Dragos said raising his cup slightly.

"Whole world is locked down tight? Defunded for repossession?" Truman asked.

"The man that hire us to do jobs wants us to do more. We are in the repossession business, brother. He give us a list of things he wants," Tullia replied.

"He'll pay us money? What good is that now?" Truman asked.

"Colonies are still funded, the collapse did not shut down the moon or Mars, but we need input for navigation computer to dodge military satellites to break orbit. Calculations are too complex for normal computer," Tullia replied with a nod.

"This man, this Uroboros, will give us money and the trajectory. He says we should meet him in Helsinki for this. Do not worry, we are wary and brought many friends and their guns in case he tries to double cross," Dragos said, again filling Truman's cup with more coffee.

"And then, we can go into space and make real money on the trade routes?" Truman ventured.

"Yes." Tullia smiled.

They stood together after sharing their meal and walked into the frigid confines of the cargo hold. Truman looked down at the Mechanic they claimed to have found, his hands and feet wrapped in a grayish foil. He looked back at them from beneath long white hair and a beard to match.

"This is the Mechanic. He won't speak, so I've taken to calling him Mr. Frumples for the time being," Tullia said gesturing to Matthias.

"What if he will not cooperate?" Truman asked.

"Our employer, Uroboros, has said that he will provide us with the necessary incentive," Dragos replied.

Their prisoner suddenly began to laugh. It was a hearty laugh accompanied by the shaking of his head, his long hair almost reaching to the ground. Tullia looked at her brothers somewhat startled as this was the only sound she'd heard him make in two months.

"What, you know something, Mr. Frumples?" Tullia asked. She knelt down next to Matthias.

Matthias just looked at her with a smile, mirth dancing in his grey-blue eyes. To Matthias, she was just a brown haired girl in a flight suit that did her best to not let everyone around her know she barely knew what she was doing. She could barely fly the commercial craft she'd stolen and the navigation computer was going out.

"Would you like some flying lessons?" Matthias said.

Tullia sneered and delivered a solid kick to Matthias' face, her work boots giving him a wide gash across his forehead.

"What are you doing? Man was very specific, that we could not hurt this man," Dragos exclaimed trying to get control of his sister.

Tullia fought her way free of her brother's grasp and stormed out of the cargo hold.

"You should be more careful. Sister does not take insults so well. None of her boyfriends live very long for this reason," Truman joked.

Matthias just smiled at them, his teeth bloody from the blow he'd sustained. Dragos and Truman walked back outside together, taking their time down the icy loading ramp. Truman turned to his brother once they were alone at the edge of the clearing.

"Thank you for not telling others about how I botched the job," Truman whispered.

"You loved that woman?" Dragos asked, already knowing the answer.

"Yes, I loved her. I wish you could have heard her sing," Truman said, fighting back tears again.

"You shot our cousin. That was hard to square with everyone," Dragos replied.

"He was going to sell her to a skin merchant! He did not consider my feelings," Truman replied tearfully.

"We have many more cousins, what is the loss of but one? Love is more important than job," Dragos said, patting Truman in an ardent attempt to console him.

"Love is more important than job?" Truman meeting his brother's gaze.

"Don't you think so?"

Truman nodded, still numb from everything that had happened. He was glad his brother was there to give him perspective in his darkest hour. He was thankful he had the love of family to give him strength to persist after the loss of true love.

"I love you, Dragos."

"I love you, too, brother. Let's find you some clothes, you look both cold and ridiculous."

"Thank you."

Meanwhile, Tullia crouched down beside Matthias after everyone left. The anger across her face melted away instantly after making sure the hold was clear. She turned Matthias' face toward her and looked at the gash in his forehead.

"Sorry, but you cannot talk to me like that in front of my brothers. Earning their respect is hard enough without you trying to make me look bad," Tullia said, dabbing at the wound with a cloth soaked in black vodka from her hip flask.

"I was serious. Do you want to me to teach you how to fly this thing?" Matthias asked. "Or do you want your brothers to find out you barely know what you're doing?"

Tullia looked at the white haired man and wondered what he would look like with a shave and a trim. She couldn't have her brothers thinking she wasn't able to handle herself, but she nearly put the transport into the side of a hill getting here. She looked down shamefully at her flight suit, two sizes too big, and despaired for a moment.

Dragos and Truman came into the hold looking for her. Dragos could tell something was wrong, but knew better than to just ask his sister. Truman stretched, breaking all the seams in his coveralls, then smiled.

"Fits better now," he reported, rowing his arms back and forth.

"Brothers, I must tell you something," Tullia began slowly.

"Yes?" Dragos said, adopting his most serious face.

"I can only barely fly this transport. Navigation computer has done most of the work, and when I fly alone I am unsteady, unsure," Tullia began.

Matthias looked on, stunned at her admission. Dragos and Truman looked at one another then back to their sister, their faces like stone.

"Mr. Frumples has offered to teach me how to fly transport, but I could not do such a thing behind your backs. I do not know what to do," Tullia said, her face turning bright red.

Matthias looked up at Dragos, fearful of what he might do. He was a hardened FLF fighter who did not accept weakness in others or forgive the same. Truman stood beside him, his face hopelessly impassive.

"Fortunately, sister, I know what to do," Dragos said kneeling down next to Matthias.

Matthias looked up at Dragos. The young man seemed lost in thought for a moment as if he was trying to set everything into its proper place mentally.

"You can teach my sister to fly?" Dragos asked Matthias.

"This is an old style freight hauler, designed to work off the grid before all SATNAV went global. I'd have to look at the engine core to tell if it's a Mark III or Mark IV. It's a large VTOL capable ship with two cargo chambers sixty feet in length, 102 inches wide, and 13.5 feet tall, each allowing the vehicle to carry 160,000 pounds gross weight. They require a single pilot and have quarters allowing up to eight other crew members," Matthias said.

"I know what it is," Dragos said smiling. "Can you teach my sister to fly?"

"CGG standard is eighty training hours for one of these. I can teach her to be an ace pilot in forty, but not while sitting restrained in the cargo hold," Matthias replied.

Dragos pulled the grayish foil meant to dampen Matthias' powers off his hands and clasped them with his own.

"If you do this, you will never fear anything from my people again. I will let you go, no questions asked," Dragos said.

"What about Uroboros? Won't he be mad that you let the Mechanic that is supposed to open all those doors for you go?" Matthias asked.

"To hell with this Uroboros. Sister's happiness is more important. She has wanted her own ship, like our father, our whole lives. It is all she wants. You will help me give this to her, yes?" Dragos whispered, locking eyes with Matthias.

Matthias was taken aback by the warmth Drago had for his sister. It was as if he would forsake the whole world and everyone in it for her. It reminded him of someone else he knew.

"Yes, I'll help you," Matthias said, holding up his shackles.

"Do you want Mr. Frumples stitched on your flight suit? Or should we call you some other name?" Truman asked with a smile.

"I'm Matthias."

Dragos stopped dead in his tracks.

"I know you," Dragos said, the color draining from his face.

"I would imagine everyone in the FLF movement does," Matthias replied.

"You know me then," Dragos replied, his siblings looking to each other and shrugging.

Matthias merely nodded.

"Then you know what I will do to you and everything you love if you do not hold up your end of the bargain," Dragos said, the corners of his mouth drooping.

"I also know you are a man who keeps his word. I'll make your sister the best pilot I possibly can, then I walk away. We still have a deal?" Matthias asked as he rubbed the feeling back into his wrists.

"Truman, Tullia, if something happens to me, make sure that my oath to this man is kept," Dragos replied.

"I will make sure of it, brother," Truman said, unnerved slightly by the passion behind his brother's words.

Tullia nodded slightly, taking a quick drink from her hip flask.

"I think it best that you follow through with Uroboros' plan to pick up and provide me incentive with regard to the mission," Matthias said. "We need to buy you as much time as we possibly can before he realizes you aren't going through with the job."

CHAPTER 6

Revelation Machine

The airport was crowded with travelers, most trying to leave the chaos as protestors clashed with riot police across much of the city. Matthias paused just outside of customs to gaze up at a large view screen displaying the local news. The smiling correspondent reported that several hundred riot police were clashing with less than a thousand protestors. Matthias new it was far more dire, with protestors numbering in the hundreds of thousands and that every soldier, police officer, and private military contractor the CGG could muster was attempting to restore order.

Matthias blinked and looked away from the screen to his mobile. He would be late if he didn't hurry. He had to move through the airport like everyone else, in just enough of a hurry to look authentic, but not frantic, even if he felt frantic. National security agents were at every corner and CGG pattern drones hovered in the rafters, multitudinous cameras pointing in every direction. The whole airport was a surveillance minefield. Walking as one would normally walk would be dangerous depending on how much documentation the government had on you.

The outside of the airport was a swarm of people moving mostly toward the airport and only a trickle trying to leave. Every cab driver and public transportation technician, pilot, and mechanic was on strike leaving people to walk or ride a rusty rickshaw from place to place. The air was thick with cologne and bawdy shouting as scalpers stood along the rows trying to sell tickets to Hong Kong, New York, Amsterdam, and other places reputed to be free of the fiscal chaos engulfing places like Brazil, Peru, and much of South America. Matthias wished he could tell the people trading away all they had for a ticket that there would be nowhere to run.

Keeping to the main streets and out in the open, Matthias traversed the strictly controlled area immediately around the airport. Moving with the crowd, keeping your head down, and being predicable was the simplest way to fool surveillance drones and systems. The checkpoint felt like a formality as the CGG border patrol agents had to process a hundred people a minute to keep people from rioting or trampling each other. There were no portable bathrooms and thousands of unhappy people to contend with.

The city air was unusually clean with almost seventy percent of the vehicular traffic grounded due to the strikes and unrest. Matthias breathed it in deeply, looking toward the sun that was usually just a blurry haze. He'd been to the region many times, but always as a tourist. There was the staccato of gunfire in the distance and the low thrum of sonic anti-protestor weapons being deployed. The night would certainly bring bloodshed as the local authorities were scheduled to meet and pass legislation further outlawing demonstrations and political action against the established CGG-backed government.

The merchant squares were full of individuals selling bottled water at outrageous prices and tarp material for tents. One could barely hear the shouts over the footfalls of the crowd as it moved through carrying with it families, individuals, and soldiers tasked with keeping order. Matthias paused under the overhang outside a shoe store to check his mobile. The local networks were choked with traffic as everyone was desperately trying to check mail, make international phone calls, and make travel arrangements.

It looked as though his meeting was being pushed back, which came as no surprise. Traveling the city would take anyone, regardless of their means, quite a bit of time. It took hours to reach the meeting point, a small cafÈ near an industrial complex beneath a towering housing project. Everything in the area was in various stages of construction, with only a few of the older parts of the original neighborhood remaining. Matthias stepped into the packed cafÈ and took up the only open seat where two other men were seated.

"Okay if we share a table?" Matthias asked in his best Portuguese.

"We saved you a seat," one of the men replied in English.

"Ah, thank you."

The man was younger than Matthias thought he would be, and distinctly North American from his shoes to his shoulder bag. His associate looked well-traveled, and bore obvious cybernetic augmentations. Matthias could see he was uncomfortable which means they probably knew more about him than he'd have preferred.

"I'm Ashton, and this is my associate, Perfidy," the younger man said, offering Matthias a still covered cup of coffee.

"Unfortunate name," Matthias remarked.

"I'm an agent of misfortune generally, except for today," Perfidy replied, smiling weakly.

Ashton shifted as if uncomfortable for a moment, then turned to look about the room for a moment. There was an array of dirty coveralls and bearded faces, greasy hands and dust covered boots. Satisfied they could speak freely, Ashton turned to Perfidy.

"Still no electronic surveillance detected. I think we're good to proceed," Perfidy said with a nod.

"The work you've done for us has been exemplary, but I'm sure you are already aware of the scope of your talents?" Ashton began.

Matthias gave a slow single nod to the affirmative.

"We're aware that you engage these internships as a cover for your other "activities," and our employer has known from the beginning," Ashton continued.

Matthias moved to stand, but Perfidy grasped him tightly by the arm. Matthias tried to will the cyborg to release him, but the psychic countermeasures in place made him momentarily dizzy.

"There's no reason to be alarmed, and you are in no danger," Ashton said abruptly swiping Perfidy's hand from Matthias' wrist.

"There's a high bounty for..."

"Hssst, we're not here to talk about that," Ashton said, turning his gaze to the room nervously.

"What do you want?" Matthias asked, crossing his arms.

"Our employer wants to put you in charge of your own project, full creative control and you would answer only to him, through me," Ashton explained.

"To what end? Who do you work for?" Matthias asked, suddenly very curious.

"I work for a single investor. He would like you to continue your work in creating a stable intelligent agent for commercial use," Ashton explained, wiping sweat from his brow with a napkin.

Matthias smiled slightly, wondering how much Ashton's employer knew about his previous employment. There were already secretly maintained intelligent agents in play, and making more was strictly prohibited by law. Still, returning to his old work was deeply appealing.

"What you're asking me to do might be impossible, not to mention illegal," Matthias stated taking the lid off his coffee.

"We know with certitude that it's possible to make an intelligent agent," Ashton said, raising his eyebrows and meeting Matthias' gaze. "And, my investor plans to have the necessary permits and clearances by the time you have a product. It isn't illegal to be in the act of development, only to house actual intelligent agents of certain capabilities."

Perfidy held up a hand, then turned his head sharply toward the window scanning the crowd with his augmented eyes. Matthias and Ashton quietly drank their coffee and waited nervously. After a few minutes, Perfidy nodded and put his hand back on the table.

"We're good, whoever it was moved on," Perfidy reported.

"How are you sure creating a commercially viable intelligent agent is possible?" Matthias asked.

Ashton seemed to pause as if to choose his words carefully.

"It is as though such a thing was written into the stars," Ashton said sending his eyes skyward.

Matthias chuckled.

"Would I be able to continue working remotely? I have obligations," Matthias explained quietly.

"My investor has requirements relative to your time to meet certain milestones on time. Everything is up for negotiation, of course."

Matthias lowered his gaze for a moment to give the impression he was giving the matter thought. He already knew what he was going to do, and how he would do it. Creating the illusion of deliberation was important if he was to negotiate the terms he wanted. It seemed to work, because Ashton rubbed his face wearily then pushed a slip of paper across the table.

Matthias put his hand out on the table covering the slip of paper and held it there for a second, lowering his head to look in Ashton's eyes. Ashton blinked for a moment, looking down at Matthias' hand. Perfidy just smirked at the quiet game the two were playing, having seen the shameful display many times before.

Matthias turned the slip of paper over and gazed at what was written on it. His eyebrows went up, ruining his best poker face. Matthias slid the paper back across the table. He quickly withdrew his hand ignoring Ashton's smiling face.

"You were going to say no, but now you aren't sure. Am I right?" Ashton asked.

"I think you people know a little too much about my business," Matthias replied, looking over at Perfidy nervously.

"This meeting was supposed to just be an alibi for your other activities in the event you were questioned. With my employer, very little is ever as it seems. I can tell you with certitude there will be no consequences if you decline. But, I'd think real hard about saying yes as well," Perfidy warned, folding his arms.

"I'm not the only one who should engage in some careful contemplation. What if I get caught and you get caught working with me? We'll all die in prison. Is your investor, employer, whatever, good with that? Just because I take a commercial gig doesn't mean I'll cease in engaging in my own form of activism," Matthias whispered, leaning over the table.

"You do a pretty good job of obscuring your age, and an even better job of erasing your past. You already have all the tradecraft to avoid all but the most careful detection, the sort no one can escape. They started requiring 'mechanics' to register with the CGG years ago, but you've even evaded that somehow. It leads one to make leaps of logic. While I and my associate here had no idea what he meant, our investor wanted it conveyed that he knows who you are," Ashton explained calmly, stirring more sugar into his coffee.

"Everything you think you know about me is based on the educated guesswork of your silent partner? I would like to know, do you trust him or her?" Matthias asked.

"It's a he, and yes, I trust him," Ashton replied.

Matthias turned and looked at Perfidy expectantly.

"No, but I don't trust anyone. Trust is an occupational hazard for someone like me," Perfidy stated, keeping his gaze locked to the crowd outside.

"That's how I work as well. I don't tend to trust anyone, either. Instead, I collect the necessary assurances to make sure that both parties don't end up at the sad end of the arrangement," Matthias said, leaning back in his chair.

"Then go about your business today and think about what sort of assurances you would require, or collateral if you will, to proceed," Ashton said collecting his things and standing from the table.

Matthias watched them leave, still shaken by what he'd heard. He'd dwelled in the shadows for a pair of decades at least, no one even shining a light in his direction during that time. He felt like a ghost resurrected as he considered what he'd seen written on the scrap of paper. He wasn't worried so much about the people he knew of that could make such an offer. It was the people he may not know of that scared him more.

São Paulo grew smokier as the afternoon arrived, but not with the exhaust of vehicles or the hum of industry. It was revolution that filled the sky with black smoke and the air with noise. The restoration district bore the scars as cobblestones had been pulled from the street and used as projectiles. Shattered barricades and an orphaned riot shield sat atop rubble at the corner where grand festivals once entertained a peaceful populace. Matthias walked through neighborhoods untouched by the violence and places that still burned with the anger of the people.

His next appointment wasn't remotely close to where he'd met attended his job interview, and his feet ached by the time he arrived. The government controlled currency exchange sat in a strictly controlled area with high fences, control points, gates, and hundreds of special government police. He stopped to check his mobile before proceeding toward the checkpoint.

The guards were wary, but not overly vigilant as riot police had kept the unrest contained at least ten blocks away. Matthias adopted his most friendly demeanor as he approached, doing his best to look as he was, a simple tourist. Cameras turned slowly back and forth from the top of the checkpoint structure, itself a special police precinct with three floors and probably four dozen rooms, offices, and cells. Surveillance drones hummed as they hovered overhead every fifty yards or so along the fence.

"Hello, I was wondering if the exchange was open today," Matthias asked in his best Portuguese.

"Yes, but only to banking officials and repossession agents. May we see your credentials?" the guard asked, shouldering his rifle and beckoning for Matthias to approach.

"Absolutely," Matthias said, pulling out his mobile.

Matthias stepped up to the fence and waved his mobile over the sense installed beside a keypad that controlled the gate. The guard inside the post nodded, and the gate began to slowly open. Matthias stepped slipped through the gate and traversed the remaining distance to the checkpoint. The guards looked in his shoulder bag and used a wand to look for large metal objects on his person before allowing him to proceed.

There were few workers on site, and most of the commercial exchange buildings were occupied only by security personnel. The currency exchange was the exception, with repossession agents and financiers barely letting the front doors rest as they came and went. Matthias was almost to the currency exchange when an explosion sent the outer fence between checkpoints crashing down. There were shouts and the audible hum of drones being deployed overhead.

"Too soon," Matthias muttered under his breath.

He hurried to the exchange, managing to get inside before the doors swung shut and locked in response to the chaos outside. The building quickly went into lockdown around him, sending up cries of exasperation from the exchange floor where currency exchange workers were trying to make a meager living. Another explosion shook the building, this time from further away.

Matthias wasted no time heading for the nearest terminal. He pulled code he'd uploaded remotely from the network and executed it, watching it compromise all but the physical countermeasures. There was little he could do about those, but the information he and his compatriots desired would be his in moments. As his code resolved, the physical countermeasures went down, leaving the government network utterly helpless.

He gazed at the terminal for a moment, wondering how it had happened. Matthias had his answer a moment later when someone from outside the network used his backdoor and the flaw his code created to begin manipulating the currency records for the exchange, making small changes in the metadata for each. Whoever it was, they weren't stealing or even doing something that would immediately profit anyone in particular. Whatever they were doing was part of some very large picture Matthias hoped he would never see the whole of.

Matthias used his increased access to defund secret prisons holding political prisoners and to close them outside of regular protocols. He could almost hear the cell doors holding old allies swing open in the distance. There was so much more Matthias would have liked to have done, but there was no time. Even as he finished collecting the intelligence he'd been sent to acquire, the physical countermeasures reasserted themselves, blocking his own psychic abilities and any further meddling.

Stepping away from the terminal he moved to the exchange floor to file the bogus papers he'd brought with him to solidify his alibi. By now, the protestors were on the grounds pushing past the ruined fences outside. Special government police would be making hasty decisions and they would have to open the buildings, even just for a moment, to retreat within. Matthias exited the exchange floor as the steel plates began to recede from the doors and windows, allowing government workers and police to shelter inside.

Matthias slipped out a bathroom window and dropped to the ground, his ears assaulted by the chaos of riot police and angry citizens clashing across the once unstained exchange square. The air was thick with tear gas and smoke, and it would be minutes before an opportunity to escape the exchange grounds would appear.

Stepping into the crowd, Matthias took out his hat and placed it over his mouth doing his best not to breathe the tear gas. He would need all the lung capacity he could muster. He turned in the direction the crowd was marching and chanted alongside them. Every few moments he stepped backwards, slowly making his way toward the gap in the fence. People pushed past him carrying stones, old hunting rifles, and hand painted signs voicing their displeasure. The streets beyond the gap were filled with standing protestors, each waiting their turn to occupy the exchange and voice their distress at the recent change to governmental fiscal policy.

Matthias felt a twinge of guilt at being able to do little in changing the situation for the average person around the world. Most people were born into debt, their parents not being able to even afford to bring them into the world. Little he did would change that any time soon, but he could certainly see that they were avenged, and that the people who stood to profit lived comfortably in fear of the radicals and revolutionaries that opposed them.

The protestors, armed with stones, beat on the steel plates that had turned the buildings into bunkers. The din was fading in the distance as Matthias walked along the main road leading into what used to be middle class neighborhoods, markets, and schools. There was nothing now but buildings the financial institutions couldn't sell having made so many destitute. It was like the whole town was curling around to eat its own tail.

Matthias reached into his pocket instinctively, his own tele-mechanical senses warning him he was about to get a call. A moment later the phone began to vibrate in his hand, the call coming in via a heavy intelligence grade encryption. He let it ring a couple of times before bringing the phone up to his ear.

"Hello?"

"Matthias, its Ashton."

"Well, this is a surprise. I figured it would be me giving you a call. Where are you?"

"I'm not far away actually. Would you like a lift to wherever you're heading next?"

Matthias let the hand holding his phone fall to his side, cursing under his breath. He waited for a moment to calm his nerves before bringing the phone back up to his ear.

"You're tracking me somehow. I don't like being tracked," Matthias said, looking around at the rooftops and windows immediately around him.

"Actually, I'm speaking purely on assumption," Ashton replied.

"Assumption of what exactly?" Matthias growled.

"My employer made predictions about what you'd do based on previous data, calculated where you would likely be, and when. He assumed you'd be a few blocks southwest of the currency exchange by now and on your way to either Santos or Praia Grande," Ashton stated, the sound of wind or a passing vehicle barely audible in the background.

Matthias froze in his tracks. Whoever these people were, they had some sort of 'revelation machine' and were using it to predict his movements. As far as he knew, no one had developed such a thing and the notion of one filled him with terror. Ashton's employer was playing with the sorts of things that could wreck the world and steal a person's destiny from them. Such a device or program could infringe the agency of people before they even had a chance to exercise it.

"I don't understand why you need me, or my talents, with what you already have access to," Matthias replied, changing his intended course.

"My employer isn't as interested in what you can do as much as the substance of your desires. It is what you want to do with the world that interests him the most. We are not seeking just a commercially viable intelligent agent, but one that is both stable and ethical. It's probably outside my purview to say so, but my employer believes that intelligent agents should necessarily have rights and the ability to choose their fate," Ashton explained.

"Don't you think your access to certain other technologies might interfere with your goal? Outcome is everything here," Matthias replied, taking the stairs to a skywalk spanning a major traffic hub.

"Have you met this guy? He would give us the resources to create this ethical and stable intelligent agent?" Matthias asked, trying to keep Ashton on the line.

Ashton didn't respond. The line going dead a moment later. Matthias looked down at his phone quizzically then up along the skywalk illuminated by the streetlights below. A single individual walked purposefully toward him. Matthias squinted in the dark, just making out the jacket and glasses Ashton had been wearing previously. They converged on each other at the center of the skywalk.

"I've met him," Ashton said plainly, looking out at São Paulo.

"And? Who am I dealing with here exactly?" Matthias inquired persistently.

"He's an anachronism and a pack rat living in a tiny apartment filled with stacks of paper and not a single computer other than an ancient mobile he carries. He dresses like he hasn't paid attention to fashion trends for decades, but he appears to be younger than me. For someone that can so accurately consider the sum of the future, he lives decidedly in the past," Ashton said, leaning on the railing.

"How does he make these assumptions, these accurate predictions about people?" Matthias asked.

"He does it in his head, but don't ask him for stock picks or to read your palm. I don't think the way he thinks allows for him to collect the whole of a thing he isn't intensely interested in," Ashton answered with a smile.

"You've looked into him?"

Ashton laughed. "Yes, I did my due diligence with all my investors, and I turned down his offer initially. Eventually, he just circumvented my attempts to avoid shadowy individuals by creating an impressive array of covers and corporate fronts for his desires. I think he represents a large controlling interest in many legitimate businesses and institutions through stock manipulation, cash holdings, and anything else that allows him to stay anonymous. Do you think he might be CGG Intelligence, throwing a wide net over both of us?"

"No," Matthias replied, lowering his gaze slightly.

"How can you be sure?"

"I would know him already, and there would be none of these elaborate demonstrations of his abilities or intent," Matthias replied a little more calmly.

Ashton looked somewhat startled by Matthias' admission.

"I doubt we'll ever know who he really is, but he's helping my company and it sounds like you would get to do something you've never done before," Ashton ventured, hoping he'd succeeded in recruiting Matthias.

Smoke drifted by the skywalk as the sounds of evening raids on protestor camps rang out in the night. The beat of canister launchers and weapons fire could be heard as the brilliant flash of petrol bombs lit up a neighborhood not far away. Ashton looked on with disinterest, as if the scene was playing out in front of him for the hundredth time.

"I'm in. But, I'll need time to travel on occasion. I want to head my own project, pick my own people, and have a secure place to work," Matthias said after a long pause.

"I'll make the arrangements."

"You haven't already?"

"You deciding to join my firm and agreeing to all this was not a forgone conclusion. I was told it would be a fifty-fifty chance either way," Ashton said with a bemused smile.

"That's strangely comforting."

"Isn't it, though?"

CHAPTER 7

HELSINKI, FINLAND

January 22nd, 2200

Taylor's Diary, Part 4

I woke up in a dimly lit observation room in Helsinki General. The last thing I remembered was standing in the street outside a convenience store while my friends were inside fighting with some soldiers who had turned mercenary. I felt a sharp pain in my side and then nothing.

I tried to sit up, but Silverstein urged me to lay back. Ezra was there, too. I'd never seen him look so miserable. He grabbed my hand and acted like it was his fault. I looked down at the pile of my clothes lying beside me on a chair and began to cry. I really couldn't help it.

"You're safe now. Please don't cry," Ezra pleaded.

I reached over and picked up my fuzzy-snuzzy coat and looked through the bloody bullet hole in the side. I'd worked so hard on it and now it was ruined. I was beside myself with grief as I clutched my prized garment and wondered what sort of world we lived in where someone would do something like this.

"I don't have any more stuffed animals to skin so I can fix it. Whoever did this is going to pay!" I said angrily, wiping the tears from my eyes.

"Um, I think there are stuffed animals in the gift shop near the entrance," Ezra said, eyes wide.

"Pink, purple, blue, or green... this coat already has too much brown and red. Go-go," I pleaded with Ezra who sprinted off through the door.

"In case you were worried, you're okay. Dr. Labs got the bullet out of you," Silverstein said smiling at me.

"I was shot?" I asked.

Dr. Labs handed me a glass vial containing a long and very slender rifle round.

"Cool! I'll be able to make a necklace with that," I said grabbing the vial and while gesturing for my bag sitting across the room.

"Tell me about the armored transport," Silverstein asked, handing me my bag.

"What about it?" I replied dropping the glass vial into my bag alongside the rest of my extremely important stuff.

"It followed us back to the hospital like a stray dog," Silverstein said with a slight grin, obviously implying I had something to do with it.

"The onboard computer has a basic AI that can operate the vehicle in a rudimentary fashion in the event the crew is disabled somehow. Maybe it just likes me better than those thugs it was hanging out with before," I suggested, honestly not knowing why it had behaved that way.

"Okay, well when you're feeling better..." Silverstein began.

"Yeah, yeah," I said hugging him.

Ezra came back into the room nearly knocking Dr. Labs down. He was carrying an armful of stuffed animals, mostly purple. This was perfect because I already had a lot of blue and green in my coat. The purple was really going to set it off and would blend in with whatever blood I couldn't get out of the surrounding area. I couldn't believe how badly the bullet had damaged my coat.

I lifted my shirt and checked my wound for the first time. It was covered in a bandage so I started peeling it back. The doctor came over and tried to get me to leave it alone, but I told him I wanted to see. He helped me pull back the bandage and looked at the stitches crossing over my side just below my ribs.

"I don't know how you survived to be honest, you lost a lot of blood, and the tissue damage was severe.... what the... it is almost completely healed up now," Dr. Labs said completely astonished after looking at the wound.

Ezra and Silverstein looked to each other somewhat panicked.

"I've taken some illegal rejuvenation drugs. It boosted my body's ability to heal. I used to skateboard professionally," I said, totally lying my ass off.

The doctor seemed to accept that explanation and wandered out of the room to check on some of the other injured and sick still under his care.

"Whew, that was as good a story as I could have thought up. Nice one," Silverstein whispered.

"I'd think you would be used to my awesome by now," I replied twirling my finger as a signal that they needed to turn around while I dressed, which they did.

I then sat down and took a nail file to one of the purple stuffed pigs Ezra had brought me. I smiled as I turned and read the label.

"Picked out some good ones, Ezra," I replied gleefully pulling the stuffing out of the purple pig.

"Least I could do. It's my fault you got shot," Ezra moaned.

"He serious?" I asked Silverstein and laughed.

"Ezra feels responsible because he was in saving my bacon while you were out in the street alone. I've tried to tell him it could have happened to any one of us out there at any time, but..." Silverstein put a hand on Ezra's shoulder.

"Getting shot is easily among the top five coolest things that have happened to me, right beneath meeting you guys," I said whisking Ezra's little skull cap off and kissing his forehead.

He reached up groping for his little hat but I held it out of reach taunting him for a moment before giving it back. He blushed slightly and put his hat back on. Silverstein looked at me relieved.

"I'm glad you're not mad at me. I don't think I could bear it," Ezra replied.

We sat and gabbed for a while as I integrated the purple pig hide into my coat to repair the damage. I used a biological spill kit hanging on the wall to clean the blood off my fuzzy-snuzzy coat and then put it on. It was as good as new, or maybe even better. It did seriously need a little purple to keep it from looking like I was just wearing it for attention.

Eamon was in the hallway sleeping, as usual, silly bear man creature thing. I poked him with my finger and patted his head until he woke up. His eyes were just slits at first then opened wide upon catching sight of me.

"You're okay!" He whisked me off the ground, showering me with affection and bear-breath.

"Y-yeah, all better. Careful, I got shot yesterday remember? You sure sleep a lot, are you supposed to be hibernating?" I said giggling.

"Oh, oops. It's warm in here, I can't help it. I can't believe you're already feeling better. I thought you were a goner," Eamon said laughing as he set me down.

That's when I heard it; a tone indicating that someone's mobile just received a message. All the communication networks were supposed to be down. Silverstein and I pulled out our mobiles. It wasn't mine and Silverstein looked at his quizzically.

"Dark web is still operating. Apparently, I've made us some travel arrangements," Silverstein said, thumbing the touchscreen on his mobile as he read the message.

It was hard to believe any network still functioned at this point, so I held up my own mobile. I willed it to seek out whatever network Silverstein was connected to, but there was nothing. My mobile just displayed a 'no service' message.

"It came up through selected servers long enough to send me the message, then it went right back down again," Silverstein said.

"We want to trust anything that came to us that way?" Ezra asked, standing on his tip toes to see the screen on Silverstein's mobile.

"It says the arrangements were made by a Mr. Vance Uroboros and his three guests, Taylor, Ezra One, and Matthias Ericsson," Silverstein said handing his mobile to Ezra so he could read the message himself.

"It's too bad the dark web went back down. I would have liked to have checked my mail, assuming the servers where that is stored came back online, too," I replied sadly.

"You think anyone has sent you mail lately?" Silverstein asked.

"Hey, I'm pretty popular. If the communications networks weren't defunded, the email would be piling up," I replied, checking my nails.

Silverstein smiled broadly, something he rarely did anymore. I couldn't help but miss the time we spent together in Port Montaigne, even if it was a little crazy. He and I shopping at the market, dodging the corporate cleaners, and bringing him pancakes while he fixed the books at the Strip & Waffle.

I think we experience moments like that so we have at least one good memory to cling to in dark times, a point of positive perspective to outweigh the rest of the adversity in our lives. I wonder if everyone feels that way or if they just move moment to moment looking for the next experience. I wanted to know how much of what I felt and thought about was intrinsic to being human, and if humans do the same, even being human.

Hope was all we had. So far it had been all we really needed.

"Says we'll be serviced by a third party carrier. What does that mean?" Ezra asked Silverstein, handing back his mobile.

"It's a sort of code, maybe? It could mean that whoever is providing the transportation won't be a commercial on-the-grid carrier. It might be being handled by someone as underground as the dark web itself," Silverstein replied.

"What are you guys going to do?" Eamon asked.

"It is the only trail of breadcrumbs we have right now. It could be Dr. Madmar, but I doubt he would be so obvious if he just wanted to harm us. Or maybe it's one of my clones carrying out instructions I gave before losing my memory," Silverstein replied. "The message says we have to be at the latitude and longitude listed in four hours. It's eight miles from here."

"I wonder if Mr. APC outside would give us a ride," I said, touching a finger to my lips.

We walked outside together, Abbey joining us from the foyer. The APC sat quietly by the curb, its oversized treads a polite three inches away. I could remember feeling something last time I touched it, so I did the same again and closed my eyes.

Residing within was a very simple AI with roughly the cognitive features and complexity of a small child. It had only a handful of directives, none of which could be carried out because the networks were all down and its parent systems, housed elsewhere, were offline. It was scared and followed me because I was the closest thing to a network it was able to find.

The side hatch opened allowing a metal step ladder to drop down. Silverstein grabbed me by the hips and held me aloft so I could climb inside. Ezra leapt up beside me, his rifle at the ready, but the interior was empty. The controls came to life and the interior lit up as the APC's engine started up and began to idle.

"No one home," Ezra called down to Silverstein, Eamon, and Abbey.

I wasn't so sure. I placed my hands on the console at the communication officer's seat and felt my way around the internal systems of the APC. The AI was there waiting for me, a prompt opening at the terminal. I asked for his designation.

"VRSAI-013," appeared on the screen beside the terminal.

"Versa is what I will call you from now on," I instructed, willing the necessary commands to be executed.

"Versa-013, online, all systems nominal," appeared on the screen this time.

Silverstein climbed in behind me and looked around the interior.

"This thing could transport a squad of soldiers, cargo, and support crew pretty easily. Think you can get it to take us to the rendezvous point? It'd be nice to have some insurance," Silverstein asked.

"This 'thing' has a name. It's Versa," I said, correcting him.

"Does it have feelings?" Silverstein inquired, genuinely concerned he'd offended Versa.

"Versa is like a child in a lot of ways. Whoever built this APC probably designed him that way so that it would feel protective of the crew and 'need' them. It makes what those soldiers were doing all the more despicable. Versa was just doing what he thought he was supposed to. From what I've been able to gather, he doesn't want to hurt anyone," I explained, feeling very professorial all of a sudden.

"How do you know Versa is a boy?" Ezra asked me.

"By the composition of the code. Artificial intelligences are often given a gender to make them seem more accessible and friendly," Silverstein responded.

I gave him a look, indicating my displeasure.

"Hey, I wasn't trying to steal your thunder. I can know things," Silverstein said with a laugh.

"It's more than simply the composition of the code, but yes, that's basically true," I explained to Ezra.

"Will he help us?" Ezra asked.

"Definitely, but if we are going to leave he needs to be entrusted to someone that will take care of him. Without a crew, he will get lonely and despondent. He needs people," I replied.

"Abbey, can you come up here?" Silverstein shouted.

"Man, everyone gets to look around but me," Eamon said, peaking in through the bottom of the external hatch.

"You won't fit!" I laughed.

"He might in the portion designed to carry the squad," Ezra said, pointing to the aft compartment.

"Maybe if he can fit his own aft compartment through the door," Abbey said climbing into the crew compartment with us.

"Hey, this is all muscle lady," Eamon proclaimed proudly.

Abbey looked about. It was clear she'd been inside of one of these before, but maybe not for a long time. She had that nostalgic look on her face as she wandered over to a gunnery position. I had so many questions I wanted to ask her that I never got around to.

"Need some new wheels?" Silverstein asked.

"I dunno, I'd have to find and train a crew to help me run it. Is the AI still sane or has it degraded?" Abbey asked.

"Versa is fine. Even though the APC is almost forty years old, he appears to have no degradation associated with extended use. His action log is extensive too, making me think he's an anomaly of sorts, but the good kind, if that makes sense," I replied.

"Compos mentis AI's were rare back in the day. It was always good to get a vehicle that had one," Abbey said sitting down at the primary gunnery position, tapping in her old access codes.

The gunnery position complied and the aft hatch opened allowing Eamon to scramble inside the area where a squad would sit. The lights in the interior of the vehicle seemed to glow brighter as Versa's mood gradually began to improve. Silverstein sat in the pilot's seat while Ezra took the secondary gunner's chair. I shrugged and took the communication officer's station.

"Let's take Versa out for a spin. Make sure the city is safe," Abbey said, flashing what was probably the only smile I'd seen her make.

Silverstein was a fair pilot and we wandered about for an hour discouraging looters and directing people to the hospital for safety. While we did so, I began linking Versa's advanced communication's capabilities to a satellite in orbit, and created my own communication network. I then extended access to Ezra, Silverstein, and myself.

I pulled out my mobile and checked my connectivity. Everything was working fine. I could chat with Versa whenever I wanted and communicate with Silverstein and Ezra in the event we were separated. It required myself and Versa as a relays, but it worked. I startled Ezra by sending him a text.

"Oh, cool. Heh, I forgot I even had this thing," Ezra said pulling out his TI-202 mobile Silverstein had given him as a gift.

I could feel the communications routing through me, as if I was filtering them and protecting them at the same time. My own internal programing, that I couldn't even understand, was giving us a firewall of sorts. I knew it was risky to use myself to route data, but we didn't have anything else.

I asked Versa if he knew what a terrestrial AI was. He told me that he did and that he was one, indicating that the APC was his body, and the onboard systems his soul. I smiled, knowing that my own situation was probably that simple. The difference was that by virtue of his body, Versa had always knew he was an AI where my own awareness in that regard was fairly recent.

"Let's start heading toward where our transportation is supposed to be meeting us," Silverstein called out, turning the corner.

Versa rumbled along with us all wondering what we would find at the coordinates. I hoped there would be nothing, and we could just go back to the hospital. It seems like every time I get close to having a home, I would have to pick up and leave for some reason. It was getting tiresome.

I wanted a place to call my own again, friends to hang out with, and craft projects to work on. It struck me how much I didn't want the life I was leading. I wondered if Silverstein and Ezra were happy, and if they would change a thing about our situation. They seemed to roll with everything better than I did, not that I'd ever let them know I thought that.

We rumbled along a main street taking the long way because the APC was too wide for slip roads or onramps. I stopped watching the exterior on the monitor after seeing the corpse of a person who had been consumed by fire. Silverstein and Ezra chatted about whether or not he or she had been lit on fire by someone else, or if they'd done it to themselves.

There were plenty of other signs of human depravity and sorrow. Beneath a makeshift shelter in front of an old library people had gathered to swap books. For many their lives would never be the same and gave into utter despair while others are seeking a way to keep the things they cherish alive. I felt miserable that I couldn't do more to prevent this from happening, but I couldn't help but wonder if I would have been just delaying an inevitable event.

Everything must end. Civilization, like a database, is constantly writing and rewriting itself to the edifice of memory. Being that nothing is perfect, the memory gets recorded incorrectly every once in a while and over time the database will collapse under the weight of those inconsistencies and errors. Civilization is probably no different.

My ardent hope was that the seamstress, the craftsman, and the creative person would rise from these ashes to begin the process of documenting and recording mankind once more. That people would again build a culture that they would wear on their bodies, write down in books and make into the tools and contrivances of their everyday lives.

"We're here," Silverstein reported.

"We are also early," Ezra said looking about through the viewfinder from his gunnery position.

"There is a commercial class transport in the sky coming this way. It's still a little ways off, ten miles or less," Abbey reported after checking her own viewfinder.

We were sitting just beyond the edge of town beside a large six lane road that led in and out of Helsinki, surrounded by forest on either side. There was nowhere to go and not much in the way of cover if something happened. The hunter safety orange transport slowly descended wavering slightly before landing gear deployed.

"Neutral operator off-grid commercial transport. Its radio tags indicate that it has a European operating status only," I reported after fiddling about with the instruments at my own station.

"Eamon, wake up," Abbey called out toward the aft.

Eamon rolled over in the aft compartment, his huge paw waving about as if looking for the snooze button. I went back and pushed one of his eyelids back and peered down at him hoping he wouldn't freak out or something. He smiled and rose trying in vain to stretch his limbs in the compartment.

"What's going on?" He rubbed his eyes with his huge paw-like hands.

"Commercial transport is descending to land at the coordinates we were told to expect travel accommodations," I told him.

"Operator?" he asked.

"Neutral, Euro licensing."

"Mercenaries," Eamon said standing up as best as he could and checking his weapons.

The large transport had two long cargo containers attached to its belly, making the whole vehicle roughly the mass of four commercial trucks when you counted engines, crew living space, and so forth. The old ones looked like an oddly cobbled together collection of metal boxes, engines, and maneuvering jets with only a few windows and ports. It was more like a flying tomb than a vehicle.

The communications station gave off a tone indicating that someone was attempting to contact us. It took me a minute or two to figure out how to respond. I wanted to make sure the transmission was heavily encrypted before I talked to these people.

"Hello, we are here to take on passengers," a heavily Slavic sounding voice said.

"Please transmit a manifest and travel itinerary," I replied.

"Oh, hello, little girl. Is your mother or father there?" the voice replied.

My cheeks burned a little at the comment, but I let it slide.

"Manifest and travel itinerary, please transmit now," I replied, somewhat impatient.

There was a long pause.

Eventually I got a response. It was a manifest indicating that we were going to somewhere in the Arctic region. The coordinates were familiar so I sent the transmission over to Silverstein's screen to look at.

"This is where Matthias went to try to confront Dr. Madmar and disrupt his operation," Silverstein said aloud.

My heart sank.

"Let's go talk to them and see who steps out to meet us," Silverstein said as he stood from the pilot's seat.

There was really no other option if we were going to get any real answers. We stepped out with Eamon plodding along beside us. Abbey stayed with Versa to try to give us cover in the event the whole thing was a trap.

The cargo hatch to the transport opened as we trudged through the snow toward it. Several dark haired men and a woman stepped out and walked toward us. A couple of them had rifles slung over their shoulders.

"Gypsies?" Silverstein whispered.

"Hello, I am Tullia," a dark haired woman said extending her hand to us with an easy smile.

She was dressed in too-big canvas coveralls reinforced with ballistic nylon and lined with soft black felt. It was pretty clear she'd made the garment herself or someone had made it for her. The others were similarly attired with custom clothes that I envied somewhat. She looked at my own coat, her gaze lingering for a moment, but I couldn't read her reactions at all.

"Silverstein, and this is Taylor, Ezra, and Officer Eamon," Silverstein said gesturing to each of us in turn.

"Cops?" one of the larger men with a rifle blurted.

Tullia cast him a glare that would turn blood into stone, then returned to her friendly facade.

"Where are your bags? We will help you load up," Tullia replied.

"Eamon isn't on the manifest, or had you forgotten?" Silverstein said folding his arms.

"I assume he is here to check accommodations before departure. He is free to come aboard and perform his duties until we are prepping to depart," Tullia replied without skipping a beat.

"We've only got the one bag Taylor carries. She can manage I think," Silverstein said looking toward me.

I shook my head and handed it to the big fellow that seemed nervous about Eamon. His smile was clumsy but genuine as near as I could tell as he took my bag. We walked along beside them toward the transport to check out our accommodations. Tullia turned and looked back at Silverstein. As she did so I could see she had auditory implants of some sort.

"By the way, nobody calls us Gypsies anymore," Tullia said with a slight grin.

"What do they call you?" Silverstein replied abashedly.

"The only game in town currently when it comes to moving people or goods by air," she replied.

"The Romani people have a monopoly on these old commercial transports?" Silverstein asked with raised eyebrows.

"Those who were not blood we adopt. While multinational corporations collapse, a community of truckers and private shippers have banded together into shipping collective," she replied taking the first step onto the ramp leading up into her ship.

"Well done," Ezra said without malice.

I couldn't help but agree with him. That they managed to stay in the air and operate the old transports without government sanction or subsidy was a testament to their fortitude and courage. That they made a living being blacklisted from commercial terminals with access to only the very few private airfields is what gave them their sinister reputation before the shutdown. In the aftermath, they used that adversity to define themselves as something more than just being smugglers and mercenaries. They were also very snappy dressers and made their clothes by hand, something I respected. I wanted to learn at least one stitch or sewing trick from them before it was all over.

The interior of the transport was very spartan with the only things being supplies and trade goods secured to the walls with pressure poles extending from the floor to the ceiling. The wooden floors were notched with the passage of hundreds or thousands of shipments being loaded and unloaded. That's when I saw Matthias leaning in the hallway leading to the crew quarters.

He smiled and walked out to greet us, his long white hair pulled back, his beard neatly trimmed. He was wearing the same sort of clothes as the rest of the crew. He looked like he'd taken a beating recently which made me worry, but the feeling gave way to my relief at seeing him.

"Matthias!" I cried out, running over to hug him.

"Taylor, I'm glad you guys are alright," Matthias said taking a knee to return the hug.

I had so many questions for Matthias I couldn't even think straight. When he cupped my face in his hands I could tell he'd been restrained and probably kicked around by the wound to his forehead. He looked about somewhat nervously which was all the excuse I needed.

I'm not sure why but I was so incredibly angry that someone had done this to him or why I felt like I had this strange connection to him. I felt it when we first met. I imagine it is like meeting a cousin you've never met for the first time and seeing the family resemblance or something.

I turned, grabbing my bag from the big man standing next to me. With my other hand I shoved him hard sending him flying back into a wall really hard. The other crewmen were stunned for a moment as rifles began clicking into place. I willed the transport to go offline allowing the emergency lights to come back on.

"What did you do to Matthias?" I cried out, turning to Tullia.

Tullia reached out to grab me but I reversed her grip, turning her arm painfully off to one angle. She was bigger than me, and should have been much stronger, but she couldn't seem to escape my grip, the area around her arm where I grabbed her rapidly turning purple. Another crewman rushed over to grab me, but Eamon grabbed him up off his feet.

"Answer the lady's question," Eamon growled, easily lifting the man from the ground into the air.

Silverstein and Ezra stepped in beside me to look down at Tullia. I could feel Silverstein's hand on my back, his way of saying he was support-ing me I suppose. Ezra looked as incensed as I was, his claws already out.

"We were supposed to do job. We needed Matthias to do it. He make us a counteroffer, and we accept," Tullia said through clenched teeth.

"Its okay, Taylor," Matthias said at last, looking visibly stunned probably by what I'd been able to do it.

I released the woman's arm and willed the transport back into normal operation. The loading dock computer rebooted and the regular lighting came back on as the engine resumed its low thrum. The crew looked about bewildered.

I felt suitably tired from exerting myself. It took a toll on me trying to control a machine that large which lacked a central computer system controlling its operation. I was amazed that I was able to do it at all.

"We insulated the cargo hold against the psychic powers of Mechanics like Matthias. You shouldn't be able to do that," Tullia muttered rubbing her wrist.

"I'm not a Mechanic. It isn't what I did you should be most worried about, it's what I didn't do," I said angrily, tears really flowing now.

"Please, do not cry. We want to be friends. I am Truman," the big man said recovering slowly from being shoved.

I glared at him, recognizing his voice.

"I know you. You're the one who called me a little girl on the radio," I said as I glared up at him.

"My bad," he replied rubbing the goose egg on the back of his head.

"Vance Uroboros contracted them to steal several things from secure locations around the world following the shutdown. They were told where to find me in the Arctic and that they should use you to coerce me to aid them. I've made a counter offer with Dragos for other more equitable arrangements," Matthias explained.

"Why did you follow through with the arrangements then?" Silverstein asked.

"Because I wanted to make sure you guys were alright and I'll need your help keeping my end of the bargain," Matthias replied.

"Do tell," Ezra said motioning for Eamon to put the crewman down.

"They want to break orbit and conduct trade between the two colonies. Their ship is already outfitted to do so, complete with stasis chambers that will support a small crew operating the ship between Earth's moon and Mars," Matthias explained.

"So, if they've already got the ship, what do they need us for?" Ezra inquired.

"The military satellites. Without input from the ground they'll just prevent all travel between Earth and the moon. Unless..." I said thinking out loud.

"Unless, someone can make the proper calculations to stay out of range of those satellites by mapping the paths of their orbits, predicting their speed and position relative to each other, and find a window of opportunity. Each satellite also has a shutdown period for maintenance that lasts about two seconds once per day. There are also dozens of other factors to consider which would normally require an extremely complex onboard navigation system this ship doesn't possess," Matthias continued.

"So they need you to break into a defunded craft and get access to the computer?" Silverstein asked.

"That would take too long and it is far from foolproof because there are no servers on the ground to borrow processing power from. No, Silverstein, we need you to make those calculations before we depart and make the needed adjustments while in flight," Matthias replied.

CHAPTER 8

Taylor's Diary, Part 5

It was hard to say goodbye to Eamon and Abbey. It was even harder to part ways with Versa. I was glad we'd still be able to chat, at least for the length of the battery onboard. With normal usage, assuming nothing happened to him, Versa should have been active for another eighty years. I wondered if I would live so long.

We were assigned two cabins on board Tullia's transport. Matthias and Silverstein shared one, while Ezra and I took the other because the bunks were shorter. Ezra was good company. While he'd lost a lot of his childlike wonder about the world above ground, he still surprised me every once in a while. I hoped we'd be friends forever.

I had a chance to observe the principal members of the crew as they spent a day readying themselves to head back into the sky. Each was their own strange story I imagined. They often spoke to each other in a language I'd never heard, making it hard to get a sense of them, but their body language told me a lot.

Tullia seemed overly confident. Her brothers were always at her side, making it clear that she was in charge, even if it wasn't required. It was as if all she wanted was to be the captain of her own transport ship, and her brothers supported her.

I could tell by the way she did her makeup that no one had ever shown her how and that she'd grown up around men, or perhaps with a mother who was absent. She made her own clothes by hand, most of them a size too large to obscure her figure. Being the only woman on board, it was probably easier to relate to the rest of the crew that way.

None of the rest of the crew poked fun at her as a result of her gender. It was clear they feared Truman and Dragos enough that they treated her like she was one of the guys. Or, maybe they feared Tullia, and her brothers were trying to keep her from killing anyone. Still, I empathized with her a great deal, for some reason, and hoped we could become friends.

Truman seemed very sad most of the time, and always had a physical copy of a romance novel tucked in his pocket. He was socially clumsy and his jokes often fell flat, but his brother Dragos would laugh anyway. He had what looked like a group picture cut from a corporate newsletter that he looked at often, which was when he seemed the saddest.

He was big, but to see how he acted around others you'd think no one had told him so. He didn't throw his weight around and preferred to work with people and follow someone else's lead than put his own ideas forward. There was something sinister about him, though. This came out vaguely whenever he got teased.

I'm pretty sure if you went too far and made Truman angry, you'd be sorry.

Dragos was tall and thin, often leaving his long black hair down to partially obscure his face. He had a lot of what looked like military tattoos. Later on, I would discover that he had an electric guitar that he played quietly for a of couple hours a day in his cabin. He was good enough and had the look. I couldn't see why any melodic death metal band wouldn't want him.

Watching Dragos was kind of like watching a ghost. Like Ezra, he could just disappear when he wanted and, in case I hadn't mentioned it enough already, he was extremely protective of Tullia. He seemed honorable to a fault as well, doing exactly what he said he was going to do. Ezra said he had the body language of a trained killer and that he was probably an extremely dangerous individual. I didn't see it, but there was a lot I wasn't seeing I guess.

I couldn't help but like Dragos. He was extremely courteous to me, and during the journey, he made sure my clothes and the linens from the room got washed with his sister's. It was as if he thought it would be improper for a man's clothing to touch mine or something. He had a lot of weird ticks, but it seemed like he was just glad to have another woman on board for his sister to talk to.

When we did got underway, I discovered some of the deal which Matthias made. He would squeeze into the pilot's compartment with Tullia, and Dragos made sure no one was allowed nearby to see, but me for some reason. It was clear Matthias was training Tullia to fly the ship, like she'd just gotten it and didn't know what she was doing. Dragos had traded a very lucrative job working for Vance Uroboros for flying lessons for his sister.

It was so sweet I cried a little bit when all the pieces clicked into place.

"Why are you hugging me?" Dragos asked as he stood guard in the corridor leading to the pilot's compartment.

"I think you're a really nice man," I replied.

Dragos smiled weakly and put his hand on my back then looked back over at his sister.

"You know what I did then?"

"You traded a chance to make serious money so your sister would be happy and confident doing what she loves," I said wiping my eyes with the sleeve of my fuzzy-snuzzy.

"Nothing. That is what I would not do for her," he replied, the warmth in his face draining away.

"If only everyone was so loyal. My friends Silverstein and Ezra are like that," I said hoping they weren't around to hear me talking them up.

"When I was in Serbian army, we were to be sequestered. No contact. My little sister hiked through the woods to follow me on maneuvers and make sure I had food to eat when we were cut off. She did not have uniform, so she could go into places and get food when there were no supplies. She got raped doing it. It was my fault. My fault," Dragos explained, a pained expression crossing his face.

"Why are you telling me this? Seems really personal," I asked.

"I want my sister to have a friend. I want you to know things about her so you see where she has been when you talk, understand things. During a police action against smugglers, I was caught in an explosion while out in a body of water called the Iron Gate. The boat was torn apart and I was two hundred yards from shore. It was so cold," Dragos explained.

"How did you survive?" I asked, as he lifted his shirt to show me a long scar along his side.

"Little sister swam out in freezing water to where I was clinging to wreckage. She cut the straps to my equipment and let sink to the bottom of the reservoir. Then, she paddled us both back to shore and made a fire in the snow with her own two hands," Dragos explained.

"Wow," I exclaimed.

"She wants to be captain of own transport, like Papa. I will make this happen," Dragos said, his tone sounding as if the words were carved into stone long ago.

"What about Truman?" I asked, intrigued.

"When his parents and our father died in war, my mother adopted him. He is blood regardless and a good man as long as he is not made to be angry," Dragos said smiling slightly.

"You seem pretty dangerous yourself," I said pointing to his tattoos.

"When I get out of the army, I only know how to do one thing," he replied sadly.

"Play the electric guitar?" I quipped.

"Yes, I love the guitar. I wish I was as good with it as a rifle," he lamented.

I turned and watched as Matthias patiently instructed Tullia. She seemed frustrated with everything she had to learn, but with what her brother had probably given up, she was determined to learn. Matthias was endlessly patient and kind, the type of man everyone probably wishes they had as a father.

"What happened to your father?" I asked Dragos.

"Military shot down his transport thinking he was a smuggler when I was eight. Tullia was only four. They inspected wreckage and found no contraband. They gave my mother what he would make in a week and a half-uttered apology," he explained.

"You still went into the service after that?" I asked.

He smiled.

"Yes, you do what you must to feed your family," Dragos stated bitterly. "Maybe what they did to my father was wrong, but it was mistake.

Corporations were putting pressure on government to stop piracy and smuggling. Their money was more important than our lives."

"I'm sorry," I replied, feeling awful.

"It is okay. I have my revenge," he replied with a smile.

"When? What did you do?" I asked, wide eyed.

"I have my revenge every day my sister's transport is in the sky while corporate transports sit defunded at ports that previously wouldn't answer radio calls from us. Now they thank their God when they see us," Dragos replied.

The ship wavered slightly, and I could hear Tullia swear in her own language. Matthias patted her gently and gave her a moment before explaining in the most patient way possible what happened and how to avoid it next time. After Matthias was finished teaching Tullia, I wanted a go at learning to fly one of these things.

"From my perspective, I am getting better deal than Matthias. Hurting him or his friends for this man, Vance Uroboros, never felt right to me anyway. Felt too much like what the old corporation would do. Things before people - this, I do not want," Dragos said curling his lip in disgust.

"What if Uroboros is angry and comes after you?" I asked.

"Hopefully we break orbit before that happens. If not, I will kill him if he gets in my way," Dragos replied, serious like a heart attack.

I wondered what Dragos would think if he knew Vance Uroboros was already on the transport with him. I had to warn Silverstein to keep his dual identity under lock and key while we were on board. As much as I had grown to like Dragos, it was clear he would kill anyone that he thought was a danger to his sister.

I bid Dragos farewell and headed back to Silverstein's door and knocked on it. He opened it, one of Truman's romance novels in hand. I laughed at him mercilessly.

"What? There's nothing else to read," Silverstein said just a little bit grumpy.

"Let me in, I want to talk to you," I said shoving my way past.

"Um, it's the maid's day off," Silverstein stammered.

"Ha, it's easy to tell which side you and Matthias sleep on. Messy and neat," I said pointing to the chaos of Silverstein's bunk to the order that was where Matthias slept.

Silverstein sighed and sat down on his bunk, offering me a place on Matthias' side to sit.

"I just got done talking to Dragos," I said.

"Yeah? Is he the dangerous mercenary killer he looks and acts like?" Silverstein said putting a scrap of paper into his book to mark his place.

"No. He told me a lot of stuff in confidence that I'm not going to repeat. He's a good guy, however..." I began.

"Hoo boy," Silverstein said holding his face in his hands.

"I'd make sure you go by Silverstein the entire voyage and not discuss the person you were before losing your memory with anyone," I explained.

"He thinks that by turning down Vance Uroboros, he and his brother and sister might be in some kind of trouble. That's why they want to break orbit even at extreme risk," Silverstein concluded.

"Yeah, basically," I replied.

"I suspected, but that's good to know. Can we trust Dragos?" Silverstein asked.

"If he says he's going to do something, you can be certain he will follow through," I said pulling out a nail file.

"Even if that means killing or maiming people to get there?" Silverstein asked, somewhat amused.

"No. If that were the case, he wouldn't have changed the deal and worked with Matthias. I think he'd like everyone to think he's that way, but when it came down to it, the first chance he had to let Matthias go and be civilized with us, he took it," I explained.

"Y'know, you need to pick up every speck of finger nail you leave behind over there. Matthias will seriously freak." Silverstein laughed.

"He needs to be more sensitive to the byproducts of beauty. As a craftsman himself, I think he'd be more understanding," I rationalized, brushing off the covers to the bunk a little. "Seriously, given the way you are and the state of Matthias' workshop, you would be the neat one. Maybe I'm finally starting to rub off on you and ..."

Silverstein just smiled and looked at me.

"What?" I asked.

"I miss just talking with you like this. Like when we were back in Port Montaigne, when we had to walk everywhere, and you'd fill the time telling me about how I should upgrade my non-existent wardrobe and such," Silverstein said.

I looked at him. He always felt like he was older than me for some reason. Maybe it was because of how he looked when we first met. This was the first time I felt like were equal in every way, both looking across the bunk at each other.

"If someone were to come into the room right now and ask us if we were a married couple, how would you respond?" I asked, genuinely wondering how Silverstein would react.

"God, I don't know," Silverstein said laying back on his bunk.

I stood up and walked over so that I could see his eyes. He was a horrible liar and I knew I'd be able to tell what he really felt, assuming I could coax an answer out of him at all. Silverstein rolled over and looked at the wall.

"C'mon, I want to know what you'd say," I said climbing over the bunk to smother the life out of him with my fuzzy-snuzzy.

"Do I have to answer now, or will this rhetorical person wait for me to summon the right words?" Silverstein said turning to look at me.

"They'll wait," I said smoothing out his hair with my hand.

I stood up and headed for the door, pausing when I heard Silverstein sit upright on the bunk.

"What would you say if you were asked that question?" Silverstein asked, trying to turn the awkwardness around.

"I would tell them the truth, that we weren't married," I said walking out into the corridor, nearly running into Ezra as I did.

"Oh, hello, Snuzzy," he said petting my coat.

"We really do need to make you one, don't we? Maybe Tullia has cloth we can use?" I laughed.

Ezra and I walked back into the cargo hold where Truman was sitting reading a book. We kept our distance as not to disturb him. The rest of the crew was down in engineering trying to fix something or other.

"If we made you your own coat, what would you want it to have?" I asked Ezra as we sat down in some cargo netting.

"It would need to have secret pockets and it would need to be black," Ezra said looking down at the tatters he was wearing.

"Hopefully we can find a kids' coat to use as a basis," I said, not realizing that would hurt Ezra's feelings.

"Yeah," he whispered.

"Sorry, I don't remember you being sensitive about your size before," I said, trying unsuccessfully to get my foot out of my mouth.

"I'm not, but I don't know when I'll be around my own people again. Even then, I've never met a pygmy that wasn't a guy," Ezra explained.

"I'm only a few inches taller than you, there's bound to be a lady Drone close to your height. If she really cares about you, your size won't matter," I said trying to throw salve on Ezra's feelings.

"Really?" Ezra replied meeting my gaze.

"You haven't been reading Truman's ridiculous romance novels have you?" I asked.

"All the guys in those are always bigger and taller than the female protagonist," he explained.

"Ezra, what a woman fantasizes about and what she ends up taking home to keep around are rarely the same," I said with authority.

The ship lurched again, as if there had been some turbulence. Ezra looked up, his ears quivering slightly. "Sensitive" Ezra immediately vanished, and the Drone I was used to appeared suddenly as he grabbed my hand and tugged me toward the cargo bay.

"Someone's shooting at us," Ezra said looking around.

The ship lurched violently to one side. Ezra grabbed me around the waist to keep me from falling, his other hand looping around one of the pressure poles. We hung there at an odd angle as the ship began to speed up. The ship shook violently as it slowly evened out.

"Strap in, we've got a situation," Tullia said over the intercom.

"Let's head to our cabin," Ezra said setting me down.

I ran along behind him meeting Dragos in the corridor. He looked calm as he checked his rifle and motioned for us to get in our cabin. We did just that, strapping ourselves to the emergency positions on the wall just inside the door. Ezra helped me get the harness on so I wouldn't be flung about and then he calmly strapped himself in, like he'd done it hundreds of times.

I could feel the ship beginning to slow and that odd feeling you get in your stomach as an elevator descends. There was a lot of shouting outside as the ship's crew dashed about opening and closing various hatches and doors. It almost sounded like they were trying to hide things before the ship set down.

Moments later, the undercarriage of the transport opened, and the landing apparatus dropped down with a harsh clank. We set down hard, making my teeth clack together on impact. Ezra looked over at me and, seeing I was terrified, reached over and took my hand. His hand was tiny, but it felt like steel wrapped in the softest leather, his claws sitting just beneath the surface of his fingers. They were deadly weapons, but still the greatest comfort I could have asked for in that moment.

Minutes went by before we were escorted out by men sporting long black beards and wearing CGG patches. We were at the edge of what looked like some sort of airfield. The land was low rolling hills with some green vegetation, but there was virtually nothing else nearby. I couldn't understand anything they were saying.

They were especially rough with Dragos, yelling at him about his tattoos and barking questions as they kicked him around. He remained calm through it all and said nothing to them. Every time they knocked him down he would just get back up and quietly meet the gaze of whoever had hit him with their rifle or kicked him.

I looked beside me where Ezra was supposed to be, but he'd slipped his restraints and disappeared. He had his cowl up when they pulled him out of the transport with the others, I don't think the soldiers realized he was a Drone. After several minutes they escorted us back to a large concrete building that was half buried in the earth.

It was unpowered and it required two of the soldiers to get the door open. They shoved us inside, and then back to a large steel cage past several desks and terminals lit by oil lanterns. They frisked each of us, then unlocked the cage and stuck us all inside with barely enough room to even sit down.

I was terrified. Nothing like this had ever happened to me before and even with Ezra free, there were a lot of soldiers. It was dark, too. That only made my fears and anxiety about our situation worse.

"What happened?" I asked Matthias, shaking a little.

"We strayed within range of a Hungarian CGG base," Matthias whispered. "It wasn't on any of the maps. They fired conventional anti-aircraft weaponry at us so I tried to climb out of range. They got us on the radio and said they'd shoot us down if we didn't land."

"Oh no, Tullia's ship," I said almost ready to cry.

"I know," Matthias said looking around. "Wait, where's Ezra?"

"He slipped away when they were kicking Dragos around," I whispered in reply.

"Be quiet, they will hear you," Dragos hissed.

I looked over at Dragos, tears already flowing. The whole situation seemed so unfair, considering all he and his sister had already endured. His stony expression softened and he pushed his way over to where I was standing.

"You should give her a hug, she looks like she needs one" Dragos said, nudging Silverstein.

"You want one after I'm done?" Silverstein joked, the others making room so he could wrap his arms around me.

"Maybe. We might all need one, depending on how this plays out," Dragos said with a smirk.

There was some yelling at the far end of the bunker and our guards grabbed lanterns and headed over. We were left along in the dark with almost no room to even sit or lean. Matthias reached over and touched one of the terminals willing the screen to come on and give us a bit of light.

"What are we going to do?" Tullia asked quietly.

"We wait. It'll be dark soon and those poor bastards will be trapped out there with Ezra," Silverstein whispered quietly.

"That little man? Don't you mean he is trapped out there with them?" Truman said hesitantly.

"No. Ezra is from the Factory, Type One," Silverstein replied.

"Type One, I do not know what that is," Truman replied.

"I do. If they don't have proper training, they all die when it gets dark," Dragos said rubbing his blackened eye.

"Little man will kill them?" Truman replied, incredulous.

"Little man will kill them," Matthias stated plainly.

"I hope he hurries. I need to pee," Truman whispered.

Just after dark we heard gunfire and cries from outside. Tullia shivered and leaned on Dragos as he did his best to comfort her. I was somewhat unnerved, too. Whatever was going on out there was bad.

Automatic gunfire and screams filled the area sporadically for another ten minutes. In the darkness of the bunker, we could hear glass breaking, and then a metallic cry as something was pried open. Ezra appeared beside the cage, lighting one of the lanterns with a match. He was bloody, his face and hands glistening with thick crimson that dripped on the floor next to him.

"There are more on patrol. I counted bunks before I came and got you guys," Ezra said out of breath. "We should skip even searching this place and be somewhere else before dawn."

He fished around in a pocket and produced a ring of keys. After a few seconds there was a satisfying pop and the door swung open allowing us to exit. Truman ran for a corner and began to hastily relieve himself.

"Little man do good," Truman half-shouted from his corner.

Tullia bristled slightly, looking angrily at the back of Truman's head as she exited the cage.

"Told you," Silverstein said clapping Ezra on the shoulder.

"I wouldn't have been able to get away if Dragos hadn't been distracting them," Ezra humbly replied.

We did like Ezra suggested and headed back to the ship. It took us almost thirty minutes to get everything back on board and locked down. Ezra laid down in the cargo hold while everyone else loaded up. When I went to check on him I could see he wasn't alright.

"You okay?" I asked.

"I think I need something to eat," he replied.

I went to the tiny food prep room in the ship and found a package of graham crackers and went back to the cargo hold. I handed Ezra the crackers and he began to shakily eat them, trying not to stuff them all into his mouth all at once. I felt a wave of worry seeing him like that.

"Little man okay?" Truman said, locking down the last of the cargo.

"Don't call him that," Dragos and Tullia snapped in unison.

"He has a name," Tullia snarled.

"Ezra, okay?" Truman said, mindful of his sibling's anger.

"My blood sugar was crashing I think. I feel a little better now," Ezra said standing up.

"Good," Truman said smiling awkwardly, giving Ezra a peanut bar from his own pocket.

Dragos took up his rifle and turned toward the open cargo door. Ezra started out with him taking up his own recovered rifle. I couldn't help but gaze uselessly into the dark and hope a patrol didn't suddenly return.

"Where are you going?" Tullia asked.

"They're making sure this doesn't happen to anyone else," I responded, knowing what Ezra intended to do.

Dragos nodded and they both headed back out into the dark. They were gone twenty-five nerve wracking minutes and then we were airborne again. Ezra and I gathered at the porthole in our cabin and he counted down quietly as we watched the ground.

There was a bright flash from the ground, and then a shockwave that rattled the ship a moment later. We watched as the fire and smoke trailing up into the sky got further and further away. Ezra hopped down and retreated to his bunk where he stripped off his shirt and pants. I took them from him and said I'd take them to laundry for him.

"Thank you," he replied sitting down on his bunk wrapped head to toe in a blanket.

"You sure you're alright?" I asked.

"I was scared down there," he replied.

"You never been scared before?" I asked.

"I never had anything to lose that I couldn't do without. You and Silverstein are my best friends. I started to feel sick and I was afraid I wouldn't be strong enough to get you out of there before they hurt you or worse," Ezra explained.

"Everything turned out okay and I was more than scared by the way. I was terrified," I said shivering a little.

"I want to teach you how to fight. You've got the strength to use my hand-to-hand style when you get angry or scared enough. It's like the tiny nanomachines that make up your body bolster you when the pressure is really on. Y'know, like when we first stepped on this transport and you saw Matthias?" Ezra explained.

"Why do you want to do that?" I asked, gathering a few more garments together of the laundry.

"So that if something happens to me, you can fight when you need to," Ezra explained.

"Nothing is going to happen to you," I said with certitude.

"I'm old, Taylor. You and Silverstein will probably outlive me," Ezra said smiling a little.

"You don't know that for sure. Hopefully by then we'll live somewhere I won't ever have to fight," I said stepping out into the corridor.

I walked to the laundry and watched the clothes tumble about in the slim machine sandwiched between an industrial air filter and an onboard server that regulated water consumption. Matthias came in carrying some bedsheets. He sat down on the narrow bench beside me and watched the laundry for a moment.

"Is Ezra alright?" he asked.

"He's physically okay, I think."

Matthias nodded. "We were all pretty scared, except maybe Dragos. I don't think he's been acquainted with that particular emotion," Matthias replied, pressing his lips together tightly.

"Ezra wants to teach me his martial style, y'know, how to beat people up," I said looking to Matthias for his opinion.

"He wants to make sure some part of himself persists in the world after he's gone, and he wants to give you the only thing he has to give. You should let him," Matthias replied.

"We live in an uncertain world, sometimes bad things happen we can't control," I said nodding.

"Like fingernail clippings on your bedsheets," Matthias stated plainly.

"Silverstein ratted me out?" I exclaimed clenching a fist in mock anger.

"I think he wanted to go to sleep and I wasn't going to let it go," Matthias laughed.

"If you leave your sheets with me, I'll wash them," I said with a sigh.

"That's all I ever wanted. Good night."

We flew all night and into the next morning. It felt like we were zig-zagging through the sky, taking a much longer route than was necessary. I assumed it was because everyone on board was suitably paranoid about getting forced out of the sky again. I kept having to remind myself that the world had been changed forever.

The next morning we set down just inside the old Serbian border in what looked like a fresh patch of nowhere for repairs. Silverstein and Matthias were going to use it as chance to run engine tests, and the rest of the crew was out stretching their legs with Truman and Dragos. I think they left hoping for some game and a bit of firewood.

I went to the pilot's compartment where Tullia sat alone. It was early in the morning and the sun hadn't even crested the horizon yet. It was just a faint glow in the distance.

"Good morning," I said sleepily.

"Ah, hello," she replied, clearly not expecting anyone else to be awake.

"I really like your flight suit. Did you make it?" I asked, pointing to the garment she wore.

"Yes. I had to. They don't make them in my size. I can see you make your own clothes, too," Tullia replied.

"Used to be that was all I did," I replied sadly. "I had to leave everything behind. All I've got now is what I carry around with me in this bag."

"That's quite a bag, though. Did you make it?" she asked.

"No, a Nigerian immigrant working in a market I liked to frequent made this. She said that it was magical, and that it would hold more on the inside than it appeared to be capable on the outside," I replied proudly patting my shoulder bag.

"Silverstein's jacket?" she asked.

"Yeah, I made that. We got it in the same market, and I altered it," I replied smiling.

"Ezra, he wears what looks like a rubber glove and coat, but they are all torn and worthless. He is wearing child's clothes," Tullia said, as if to scold me.

"That's why I'm here actually. I'm hoping you have some material that I could use to make him a set of clothes, or at least a warm jacket," I asked.

"None of my wire forms are the right size. He is so small. He will have to come to my room so we can measure him," Tullia said climbing out of the pilot's compartment.

We went and ambushed Ezra while he was still sleeping. He looked up at us, squinting through grayish slits with his unearthly eyes. He followed along behind us wrapped in a blanket down to the second cargo container that had been converted into crew quarters. Tullia's space was the largest and she had a collection of fabric anyone would envy.

"Wow!" I said looking about.

"You like?" Tullia said blushing.

"Very much," I replied pulling out a stool for Ezra to stand on.

"Seriously, why am I here?" Ezra yawned.

"Taylor and I are going to make you pretty," Tullia said ominously.

"Okay," Ezra said with a shrug.

Tullia and I both laughed at his easy resignation. We set about measuring Ezra which was an interesting experience. He was the size of a ten year old boy but at the same time he was far more like a man. He was slender, but well-muscled and his skin felt like what you'd think a shark's skin would feel like, cold and just slightly prickly.

Tullia was mesmerized by Ezra's hair, which he usually shaved off but hadn't had a chance to. I gasped myself when he took of his rubber skullcap and threw it to the ground. He had a head full of slightly wavy snow white hair. He stood there patiently in his trousers while we took his measurements and talking to us about what he'd like his clothes to be like.

"Tough. Black. Made for utility and durability. They have to survive doing what I do, and water resistant, should I ever get back home," Ezra explained as he sat down on the stool.

"I have ballistic nylon that is black, but for the parts that must be more flexible, I have green canvas," Tullia said, sifting through one of her many piles of cloth.

"Green is good, as long as it isn't too bright. Right, Ezra?" I said.

Ezra nodded as he took out Truman's peanut bar.

"Yes, green will go with his skin, but he will need pants and a hat maybe?" Tullia replied.

"He lost the last hat I made him, and he has such interesting hair, maybe not a hat?" I said kicking his rubber skullcap under a table where it would hopefully get lost.

"A hoodie then, to keep the rain off him and his ears warm in the cold? Harder to lose, too," Tullia replied.

"A tactical hoodie?" Ezra said smiling as he finished off the peanut bar.

"Yes, we should do a whole clothing line for Drones," Tullia said with a smile.

Tullia and I worked together all morning. We talked with Ezra, and each other, trading sewing tips mostly. We talked and laughed about what we'd make after we were done making Ezra his tactical hoodie and pants, even though we knew we'd likely be parting ways soon.

"We should make Dragos and Truman jackets with the logo of your transportation company on the back," I suggested.

"I haven't got a logo," Tullia replied.

"You going to make one?" I asked.

"I have some ideas, but I'm terrible at drawing or painting. I want there to be a circle, with a branch and leaves in the background with birds just taking flight. All thick black lines. Something that would look good on the back of a jacket or flight suit," Tullia explained.

"Sounds good," I said.

"You are the only one who thinks so," Tullia said, obviously in reference to her brothers.

"Ezra, do you need some shirts?" Tullia asked. "I have many with a men's cut that fit me. They would likely fit you, too."

"Oh, yes please. Will you guys help me pick out a couple?" Ezra said looking about the room bewildered.

Poor Ezra didn't know what he was in for. Tullia must have had a hundred t-shirts and he got to try them all on to see how they would look with his new pants and jacket. We chose a blue one that said 'Varsity' on the front and a black one that said 'The Ramones' on the back.

Ezra was very pleased. He strutted about in his new pants and his tactical hoodie. Both were about fifty percent green canvas and canvas lined with ballistic nylon across the elbows, knees and shoulders. Tullia even patched his boots while I went and made us some brunch.

When I returned to the sewing sanctum with my hard-as-a-rock waffles, Tullia was hand stitching a couple of patches on Ezra's jacket. One was for an ancient band called 'Slayer'. Then she began sorting through a shoe box full of what looked like old flags from the countries that existed before the Central Global Government.

"You are from America, Ezra? You are an American?" Tullia asked.

"Yes," Ezra said after a moment's thought.

She took out a faded red, white, and blue colored flag and sewed it onto the breast pocket opposite the shoulder she'd stitched the 'Slayer' patch. Ezra reached over and ran his fingers over the patch sitting just over his heart thoughtfully after she finished.

"Okay, button it up and make sure it fits properly. If it's okay, we can begin adding the pockets to the inside you wanted," I said excitedly.

Tullia and I had made one incredible jacket. It looked really good on Ezra. Tullia cut fabric while I worked on the jacket lining to add the pockets. I think we spent more time adding the pockets than we did making the jacket. After a few alterations to Ezra's specification the whole thing was finished and it was well into the afternoon.

"Thank you," Ezra said as he threw a few punches at the air, testing out his new apparel.

"You are most welcome. It is the least I could do after you stopped those deserters taking my transport from me. You have my brother's respect. That isn't an easy thing to earn," Tullia said.

"I was just protecting my friends," Ezra replied humbly.

"Oh, and this was so much fun anyway!" I exclaimed, putting Ezra's hood up to see how it looked.

"Yes, it was," Tullia said smiling a rare smile.

CHAPTER 9

BOGOVINA, ZAJECAR DISTRICT
1:31 AM, January 25th, 2200

Taylor's Diary, Part 6

We landed in a small patch of wilderness outside of Bogovina in the middle of the night. I knew this was one of our many stops before we were to try and break orbit for the moon colony. I was anxious after what happened in Hungary.

Lawlessness seemed to abound in the wake of the shutdown, but the tiny village of Bogovina didn't seem to notice. It had power and people appeared to be heading to work in the early morning hours. I knew it was extremely unlikely, but couldn't help but wonder if the news of what had happened to the rest of the world hadn't made it here yet.

Dragos and Truman could scarcely wait for the loading ramp to descend so they could step out onto their home soil. It was cold, but there was no snow on the ground, and it was quiet save for the occasional dog barking in the distance. It was beautiful country, nothing like the concrete jungle I was used to.

Tullia came down shortly thereafter to find Ezra and me sitting on the edge of the cargo bay, legs dangling over the side.

"Good morning," she said, taking a deep breath, as if she were breathing in her home.

"Hello," Ezra said, doing his best to eat the oatmeal I'd made him.

"Where is Mr. Silverstein?" Tullia asked.

"He and Matthias are probably still sleeping. They had a late night I think, messing with the engine. They were trying to get readings for the calculations Silverstein is supposed to make," I responded.

"Seems like some very hard math. Can your Silverstein really conjure the numbers in his head?" Tullia asked.

"Probably. If he can't, he'll tell you so," I said, trying to sound reassuring.

Tullia nodded as she looked out at her brothers taking turns looking through binoculars. Usually I couldn't read her, but at that moment she looked very worried. She turned and met my gaze with a scowl. I quickly diverted my attention back to Ezra who was still furtively attempting to eat his oatmeal.

"You have to eat, Ezra," I whispered. "Who knows what might happen today?"

"I know, but I've been thinking," he responded. "If we go to the lunar colony will we ever come back? I do miss my fellow Drones back in Port Montaigne and wonder how they are doing. I don't want to leave if there is no way back."

I didn't have an answer for him. I honestly didn't know whether we would be able to return to Earth in the aftermath of breaking orbit. I knew that eventually the orbit of the military satellites would decay and that they would fall and burn up in the atmosphere, but maybe not in our lifetime.

I thought about the people we left behind in Port Montaigne and the lives Dr. Madmar destroyed in the process of pursuing his own agenda. I mourned them because each was part of the tapestry of my old life. I lived in downtown, but I lived well by my reckoning.

"What is wrong?" Truman pausing as he walked up the ramp.

"Ezra misses his family back where we come from," I replied, patting Ezra.

"I know how he feels," Dragos said, teeth clenched.

"Mama?" Tullia asked.

Dragos almost imperceptibly shook his head as if he didn't want to. Tullia wept bitterly as Dragos held her. Ezra and I looked at each other totally baffled for a moment.

"Mother's home is boarded up. Notice on the door. Something happened to her before we could return," Truman explained.

"Maybe she just moved?" I asked.

"No, not unless she was dead or they took her away for some reason," Truman replied.

"Who is they?" Ezra asked between mouthfuls.

"CGG owns most of the village, or at least they did before the shutdown of global economic system. If you miss a single house payment or do not pay taxes, they take you to a work camp," Dragos replied bitterly.

"Someone has to know what happened!" I said, wondering why they weren't going door to door trying to find their mom.

"Not so simple," Truman stated, looking over his shoulder. "Dragos is army deserter and a known Financial Liberation Front asset. I am also wanted fugitive."

"What are you wanted for?" Ezra asked.

"Murder," Truman replied. "I kill two people in prison. It was me or them."

Ezra and I just blinked at Truman for a moment expectantly.

"He was young and foolish," Tullia said at last. "He bought a car he couldn't afford and they sent him to work camp to pay what he owed after it was repossessed. You must understand, Central Global Government gave certain governments latitude to avoid being defunded in their own way. In Serbia it was work camps."

Truman just looked down, putting his hands in his pockets and shuffled his feet.

"I don't remember anything like that making the news internationally," I said.

"In Serbia, it wasn't news. Truthfully, compared to other places, we had it pretty good at home here. There were jobs to work and ways to get along provided you didn't try to live like a rockstar," Dragos explained, speaking a little louder in Truman's direction toward the end.

"I know, I was fool," Truman said indignantly.

"You just wanted what it seemed everyone else had," I said in his defense.

"If you watch TV, it sure seems that way," Truman lamented.

"So, what are we going to do? Just leave?" Ezra asked.

Dragos contemplated the answer for a moment, as if he wasn't sure himself. Truman shrugged sadly. Finally, Dragos turned to Tullia.

"It's up to you, little sister," Dragos said quietly. "Could be more trouble than we want. Do you think Mama would want us to take a risk in her behalf?"

"She would probably beat us with a stick for risking ourselves to find her," Tullia answered. "I need to know what happened to her, though. I cannot leave until I do."

"Okay. Taylor and I will go poke around in town and try to find out what happened," Dragos replied.

"What? Why you and Taylor?" Ezra asked, putting the oatmeal down.

"I need someone who speaks very good English, with American accent. Ezra and Matthias both have slight accent, and we can't risk something happening to Silverstein. Taylor with her colorful coat and hair will look like a lost tourist," Dragos explained.

I believed him, but Ezra was extremely uncomfortable with the idea.

"It'll be okay. I want to help him. If we're not back soon, you have my permission to tear the town to tiny pieces looking for me," I said hugging Ezra.

Ezra and Dragos locked eyes for a moment, as if they were exchanging a silent vow. Dragos then turned and handed Truman his rifle, two handguns, a selection of knives and, his dog tags. He hugged Tullia and then Truman, then asked me if I was ready to go. I was.

I followed him through the field to a dirt road and then into the small village. None of the buildings were the type you would see in Helsinki or Port Montaigne. Most looked to be at least a hundred years old and lacking any of the modern countermeasures against theft or terrorism. People walked past us raising their hands in greeting, wishing us a good morning, some in English when they saw me.

We walked into the police station where Dragos began to talk to the desk sergeant pointing to me occasionally. The officer came over to me and took my hand.

"I am so sorry your wallet was taken. Please, come this way and fill out a report, we'll see if we can help you," he said in fairly good English.

I sat down at the desk and distracted him as best as I could while Dragos slipped into an office and thumbed through a file cabinet. He was only a minute before he slipped back out. I filled out the report, giving as vague a description as I could. I could tell the desk sergeant wasn't going to work too hard on this based on the degree of cooperation he was receiving from me.

"Thank you. Is this contact information current, in case we find your wallet?"

I nodded.

"Is there anyone I can call for you?"

I shook my head and smiled.

"Okay, we'll be in touch. Hopefully, we can find something out today," he said trying to be friendly.

We walked back out into the street. Dragos reached back and pulled the bit of string that was holding his hair back letting it fall down about his shoulders. We went into a corner store that had precious little on the shelves. Dragos bought two cigarettes.

"Want one?" he asked me.

"Oh yes, I haven't had one for a very long time," I replied trying to remember the last time I smoked.

He lit both and handed me one. It tasted a lot like the one's Silverstein smoked.

"Did the shopkeeper have anymore? I'll bet Silverstein would like these," I asked.

"Yes. Are you and Silverstein... together? I mean are you and he...?" Dragos stammered.

"Did you really need me to come along with you? Or did you just want to get me alone to find out if I have a boyfriend?" I asked fishing around in my bag for something I could use to get more cigarettes.

"Both," he replied.

"Silverstein and I are very close and we care for each other very deeply," I replied, finding some old CGG credit slips. "Think he'll take these?"

"But?" Dragos said nodding and gesturing to the shop door.

We went inside and I bought as many cigarettes as I could afford. He wouldn't take my CGG credit slips, but after looking in my large bag of stuff, he gladly traded me twenty cigarettes for a lipstick and a bottle of perfume I didn't like anyway. He smiled, sure he got the better end of the deal.

A lot of people probably thought that things would be back to normal soon and that the CGG would just turn the lights back on any minute. The shopkeeper wasn't an optimist in this regard, and neither was I. That one civilized transaction with the shopkeeper made me incredibly homesick, and glad that I had something to trade.

"You were telling me about you and Silverstein," Dragos said as I came back out, refusing to let the conversation drop.

"We both have our issues, things that really make contemplating a relationship difficult," I explained.

"With each other?" Dragos ventured.

"With anyone," I replied.

"That is too bad. Are you sure I cannot help?" Dragos asked.

I smiled and shook my head.

I really didn't know what to tell him. I certainly couldn't tell him that Silverstein was most likely an amnesiac Vance Uroboros and that I was a terrestrial artificial intelligence. At that moment, I certainly didn't feel artificial in the slightest. It was really flattering to be wanted, and Dragos was very handsome in his own way. The hair certainly helped.

"You are beautiful, but that is not what gives you allure. I have traveled the world, met many people. Never, anyone like you," Dragos said, crushing the remainder of his cigarette into the pavement.

I offered him one of my cigarettes to replace the one he gave me.

"Gift," he said, shaking his head with a smile. "Maybe I take one later?"

"Did you find what you were looking for in the police station?" I changed the subject.

"No. It does not make sense, she isn't listed as having her home repossessed. I have a friend we can talk to," Dragos said quickly, as if he had been snapped back to reality too abruptly.

We walked to a small house just outside the downtown area. The tiny cottage was surrounded by a rickety plastic fence and painted forest green. The door opened before we even made it up the short walk to the door. A police officer stepped out into the yard.

"Bratislav?" Dragos said, obviously surprised.

"Yes, Dragos," the policeman replied in a thick Slavic accent, just as surprised. "What are you doing here?"

"I am looking for my mother," Dragos replied looking nervously.

"Relax, Dragos, relax. We killed Nikola and his brother Pavle, the village is run by man we elected," Bratislav said, holding up his hands.

"What happened to my mother?" Dragos asked, more insistently.

"She died of heart attack. We put the CGG notice on the door to deter people from looting. I knew you would come home eventually. Your mama's house should be just as you left it. I pull out anything that might spoil and covered things up for you," Bratislav explained, his hand still up in front of him.

"Why would you do that?" Dragos said quietly, still nervous.

"We all know what you did. CGG came through looking for you. Russian Mafia got nervous and pulled support for Nikola and Pavle because of it. People in the town made sure they didn't get home from drinking and we've been okay since," Bratislav explained.

Dragos was quiet for a moment.

"Who is your colorful friend?" Bratislav asked, looking to Dragos for approval to shake my hand.

"She is friend," Dragos said with a nod.

"Hello, friend," he said and shook my hand. "I am Bratislav."

"What happens now?" Dragos said, still obviously distrustful of Bratislav.

"I should show you where your mother's grave is. I just need to get my coat," he replied heading back toward the door.

Dragos reached out and grabbed Bratislav by the hand taking the handgun from his belt in one fluid motion. Bratislav didn't struggle, he just held his hands higher in acquiescence. Dragos looked around nervously, walking the police officer back into the house. Not sure what else to do, I followed him inside.

"You have gotten fat, and obviously stupid if you think I am to believe you," Dragos sneered pushing Bratislav down into a chair.

Bratislav sighed loudly and folded his hands in front of him on his lap.

"Dragos, you were hired to do a job," Bratislav replied coolly. "Your employer heard that you are thinking of backing out. You should just head back to your transport and await instructions. How did you know? My story was very good I thought."

"You always were a bitch, Bratislav. You stink like the shit you are full of," Dragos said putting the handgun into his waistband.

Bratislav nodded and leaned forward slightly.

"Again, I ask you. What happens now?" Dragos insisted.

"Past getting you and your sister to go out to the graveyard by eight in the morning, I have no idea. I'm telling you the truth," Bratislav replied.

"Who are you working for?" I asked.

"He said he is Vance Uroboros," Bratislav replied.

"Nikola and Pavle?" Dragos asked.

"Dead, just like I said. That part was true."

"The Russians?"

"I still owe them money, I'll never be out," Bratislav replied.

"I disagree." Dragos pulled the gun from his waistband and shot Bratislav in the face.

He slumped forward, blood spilling out of the steaming wound in his ruined face. I couldn't help myself, I let out a short scream before Dragos clamped his hand over my mouth. I struggled against him, trying to get away.

"Quiet, we need to get out of here," Dragos said picking me up.

When we got outside he set me down and I gave him the most betrayed and angry look I could muster. He looked sadly down at my tears on the hand he'd used to stifle me and then motioned for me to follow. He didn't have to shoot that man, and I was pretty much done following him around as a consequence.

"Please, we need to go," Dragos said.

"You can't just go around shooting people, and I swear you'll regret it if you ever touch me again," I replied angrily.

"There really is no time to explain. We need to go," Dragos pleaded, looking genuinely afraid.

I grudgingly followed, just ahead of a crowd of people coming to the cottage to see what was going on. Ezra tearing up someone who is armed and trying to hurt us is one thing, but Dragos executing someone like that was not okay. I decided at that moment that Ezra, Silverstein, and I needed to get some distance between us and these people, or Dragos at least. I wasn't sure what Matthias would say, and I didn't care. I was pissed.

"I hope you know we're done. I'll tell my friends what you did and that'll be that," I muttered as we walked through a field.

"Did you hear the way Bratislav was talking?" Dragos replied as we walked.

"No," I replied too angry to think straight.

"His accent went away and his English improved. He spoke just like someone for whom English is their first language," Dragos replied grimly.

"Yes, I guess so. I don't see how that matters," I replied.

"When I fight with the FLF we encountered people like that once in a while. They would act like someone else was controlling them. Sometimes it would be a friend we would not see for some time and then they would betray us," Dragos tried to explain.

"And?" I said impatiently.

"We could always tell because the way they talked would change. After, when we check their bodies, we'd find out they weren't real. They had mechanical parts in them, and the rest looked to have been grown in a laboratory, and then made to look like the person," Dragos explained.

A shock ran through me as I thought about how Madmar had used Russ and our friends back in Port Montaigne against us.

"How well did you know Bratislav?" I asked.

"Since we were children. Well enough to know that was not him we were talking to. Also, I could never have disarmed the real Bratislav like that, and he would never have tolerated me calling him fat or stupid. He would kick my ass," Dragos replied sadly.

"You were friends?"

"He taught me to fight in the military. Very good friends."

I had to wonder if Ezra faced the same situation with Russ when he walked into that trap going into Port Montaigne alone to find the catalyst. If Dragos was right it meant that someone was kidnapping people, replacing them with synthetic replicas, and forcing them to hurt their friends, face death, or worse. It seemed horribly inefficient, but when you needed a body double that looked and acted like the real thing, it would be incredibly effective as long as the person was afraid of pain or death.

"I know it is hard to believe, but someone is controlling these people," Dragos whispered.

"I believe you, but do you think that was the best way to handle that situation?" I replied.

"If I were being controlled like that, I would hope someone would shoot me before I could hurt someone I cared about," Dragos replied.

We walked the rest of the way to the transport in silence. Silverstein and Ezra were outside talking to Truman as we emerged from the brush. They were relieved to see me, and I was very glad to see them. Truman exchanged a few words with his brother and then walked inside the transport.

"What happened?" Silverstein asked, seeing I was a little shook up.

"One of Dragos' friends had done to him the same thing, or similar to what was done to Russ," I explained.

"Oh, this is not good," Ezra muttered.

"What happened?" Silverstein asked.

"Dragos shot him in the face, right in front of me," I said tearfully.

"God..." Silverstein said wrapping his arms around me.

Silverstein wasn't strong or fast, or even deadly. None of that mattered, he could make me feel safe like no one else could. I knew deep down he was good, and that he would never hurt me or anyone else for that matter. I hugged him back as tightly as I could, not wanting to let go.

Ezra looked suitably grumpy.

"Ezra, did you kill Russ?" I asked laying my head on Silverstein's shoulder.

Ezra looked shocked for a moment.

"No. Madmar tortured him to death wherever his real body was being stored. He told me he was being held in a plastic tube somewhere and was being used to control the facsimile of himself. It's how I knew what had happened to him at all," Ezra explained after a moment's hesitation.

"Would you have?" I asked.

"I was pretty mad. I thought he'd betrayed us. I don't think I could have, especially knowing what I know now," Ezra said sadly.

Ezra's words filled me with equal parts horror and relief.

CHAPTER 10

Golgotha

The Midtown shuttle ground to a halt at the corner. After a moment, the doors slid to the side allowing riders to exit to the street, feet clacking against expanded metal stairs. Vance waited for the folks ahead of him to exit, then checked his mobile. It had been a year since he'd been to the area and little had changed.

"This is the last stop in midtown," the shuttle driver said over the intercom.

"Okay," Vance said, knowing the driver couldn't hear him from behind the bullet-proof glass.

He stepped off, the shuttle barely waiting for his feet to touch the pavement before speeding away. The urban renewal program had ground to a halt following the recent mayor's removal from office, funding drying up alongside her reputation. Concrete forms stood unfinished, without doors or windows to complete them along one side of the road. The older buildings that had been spared the wrecking ball stood along the other side, each an illegal tenement or shelter for the indigent. A few had power, the residents probably pooling their resources for the luxury.

Vance walked purposefully toward the old market row past darkened neon signs, security fenced storefronts, and ancient vehicles abandoned by the roadside. The street was quiet enough one could hear the current traveling the power lines overhead. Trains didn't even run through midtown anymore, and the foot traffic tended to avoid all but the most direct routes to public transit. Walking off the beaten path was dangerous after nightfall.

Fortunately, his destination was in sight and he slowed his pace to take a look around. He circled the block and came at it through an alley. Vance looked up at the rooftops and the windows that were not boarded up, but everything seemed clear. He walked up to the only obvious entry and looked for a doorbell or some sign he was in the right spot.

The exterior of the building was old, appearing to have been painted over several times. Once, it was probably a commercial property that housed several businesses, all linked together by a single storefront and a hallway. Once, it probably possessed a lot of the local personality, showcasing independent merchants and helped to create a sense of community to the neighborhood. Those days were long past.

The door to the place was locked and lacked any discernible keyhole, an odd sort of security measure. Vance backed up to the edge of the sidewalk and looked up at the plain brick building to see if there was a window that hadn't been painted over, or some other means of egress. He decided to wait, pulling out a cigarette and lighting it. About halfway through his third drag, there was a sound from behind the front door, a steel bolt sliding to one side.

The door opened slightly, allowing half of a man standing to the interior to be seen. "You must be Vance," the man said, beckoning for him to step in off the street.

Vance looked in either direction along the empty street before heading inside. The hallway was cramped, bookshelves taking up the shoulder room along both sides. The tile floor was ancient, showing signs of having been stripped and waxed hundreds of times. Vance watched the thin man with greying hair secure the door behind him, sliding a thick bolt into place.

"Are you Cal?" Vance asked, looking from the door to the books on the shelves.

"I am. We are glad you could make it."

Cal was dressed in simple clothes decades out of style, and as old as the building. His shoes and pants were well worn and faded, but still serviceable.

"What do you do when you have to go out?" Vance asked, gesturing to the door.

"Oh, I don't go out. People might recognize me," Cal replied turning on the hall light.

Vance looked at Cal, sure he'd seen him somewhere, but where exactly eluded him for the moment. He followed Cal along through what looked to be a private library of sorts, full of books he'd never seen, each with irregular binding. It was as though every book within had been bound by hand and arranged in a way that only the owner of the collection understood.

"Interesting collection you have here," Vance remarked, passing his hand over the spines of several books.

"Yep," Cal said, pausing for a moment to look around wistfully.

"Your message was pretty vague. Maybe you can tell me what this is about?" Vance asked.

"This way, please," Cal replied, leading the way to a parlor in the rear.

There were booths with round tables, like one would see in a diner, and a small kitchen. A pair of elderly gentleman worked in the kitchen while a trio of individuals waited for them at table set up in the center of the room. There was a man younger than Cal, a woman in her 50s, and an individual wearing a thick robe with many veils. Cal pulled out a chair for Vance and then sat down himself.

"Alright, I'm here, tell me what this about," Vance said, sitting down and smoothing out his jacket.

"This is about our most august assembly, of which, we are all part," Cal began.

Vance bowed his head and smiled.

"Not what you expected is it?" Cal stated without emotion.

"It is rare for us to see each other, and I doubt this many of us have ever been in a room together, speaking face to face. We each value our privacy, the state of which, integral to keeping out of each other's way," Vance whispered harshly, somewhat angry.

Cal turned to the others at the table and gestured to the individual wearing robes and veils. "You could have obscured yourself as our colleague has, come with your precious privacy in mind," Cal replied, his tone growing cold by the last word.

"I doubt the veils and robes have anything to do with privacy," Vance muttered.

Vance looked around at the table exchanging a glance with each person sitting there. He could guess who the man and woman likely were by their dress and demeanor, but Cal and the person wearing robes and veils were a mystery. He knew they were probably like him, still out in the world trying to push an agenda as opposed to dwelling strictly in the shadows.

"Is this where you tell me what this is about?" Vance said at last, breaking the silence.

Cal let out a long sigh, then nodded. "We've reviewed your plans for the future, what little you have revealed to the gathered minds of our fellowship."

"And?" Vance replied.

"We would like you to reconsider some of what you intend to do. There are some of us who would be adversely..." Cal paused, considering his words carefully.

"Some of us have collected vast wealth in our lifetimes. They like the power they have and delight in watching others starve when they have more than they could ever spend or use," Vance stated plainly.

"That is certainly one way of looking at it. Others would contend that they use their influence for the good of mankind, acting as stewards and guardians," Cal rebutted, clasping his hands together.

It was then that Vance remembered where he'd seen Cal before. Not that he had any expectations to begin with, but he had a feeling the gathering was going to take a hard left. Vance turned and looked at the woman, holding out his hand to her. "What would you say, Cerise? Of everyone here, you know more about what I'm trying to do than anyone. Your own agenda is not so different."

"You would ask us to believe you could safely level the ocean floor, filling in the vast trenches and leveling reefs so that the whole of it was a flat plain. Nature contradicts hubris relative to the scale one harbors such ambition," the woman replied placing her hand on the table as if voting her conscience.

The table grew silent again, everyone but the veiled individual growing very still. The individual wearing the robes shifted forward in their seat, and began to speak with a voice little more than a cracking hiss. It was as if each word was coming from an old vinyl record player. Gloved hands with wrists obscured by white silken wrappings gesticulated as it talked.

"We are not all here to voice our concern with your plan, Vance Uroboros. I have come to not lend you aid, or contribute, only to voice my support. Not everyone among us would deny you the rights granted by our unique condition. Do as thou wilt."

Vance looked on somewhat startled, as Cal turned to face the individual in the cowl and veil with a harsh demeanor. The others at the table sat back in their chairs, but the moment was interrupted by the two elderly cooks bringing food to the table. They ate together in silence, the veiled individual taking only meat with a gloved hand and a silver fork.

"This meeting was a mistake," Cal announced.

"I disagree," the younger man at the table replied, his words permeated by a thick accent.

"I do not see Vance diminished in his desires, or likely to change the course of his affairs," Cal said, speaking for a moment as if Vance wasn't there.

"Ah, but he must ask himself many questions now. If there are those that support him in voice, but will not lend him a limb to that end, he must know there could be the opposite amongst our number as well," the young man stated, turning his dark eyes toward Vance.

"Bring it, Kasra" Vance snapped angrily.

"You know my name? Then you must know all about me as well?" Kasra replied, reveling in the horror afflicting Cal and Cerise as they came to realize whom they were sharing a table with.

"You're a thug, and a murderer that uses our 'condition' to enrich himself," Vance replied, taking a last bite of his ham steak.

"You speak as if what you intend to do is so noble, and that it isn't feeding some needy part of you. You would pass judgment on the whole world, make decisions for other people that are not yours to make. You and I are no different," Kasra stated plainly, dabbing the corners of his mouth with a napkin.

"Cal pointed out that there were some who looked upon what they had as a stewardship or responsibility. We all have talents we don't understand, but mine are singular, specific to given endeavors. I can't deny my own capacity to calculate outcomes any more than you've denied your capacity for violence and depravity," Vance replied, scowling.

"I've seen some of what you're proposing to do. This is much more than merely calculating outcomes. You are trying to create outcomes, control things that are perhaps not meant to be controlled," Kasra said, looking lasciviously at Cerise.

Cerise looked away, and down at her food. Kasra chuckled, turning his gaze toward the individual wearing cowl and veil, his eyes slowly moving down to the gloved hand resting on the table. He smiled wickedly and leaned in close trying to peer through the veil to the eyes he assumed lay somewhere beneath.

"You are the only one whose identity I have yet to deduce. All I can see so far is that you are a woman by the dainty way you wield a fork. Since we are all now acquainted, perhaps you could tell us your name?" Kasra cooed, his words dripping with mock sweetness.

"I am called Golgotha..." the veiled individual hissed, lunging at Kasra.

The lights flickered and died as Golgotha snatched Kasra from his seat. There was the discernible sound of bones and joints popping as Golgotha's limbs rapidly elongated and her stature grew. In the fading light, Kasra drew a long curved blade in his defense, stabbing wildly at his attacker. Cerise cried out as the table went crashing to the floor in the struggle. Vance wrapped an arm around Cal and pulled him away quickly, trying to avoid the battle entirely. He took a blow to the face for his trouble, tumbling to the ground.

The lights blinked out completely as Kasra's screams were cut off by the sound of wet meat being separated from bone and something spattering across the tile floor. Cal blindly pulled a handgun from his waistband, but it was quickly dashed from his hand as Golgotha rose to her full height, towering over him in what dim light remained. Cerise fled for the kitchen, sprinting past the stunned cooks to where she hoped a back exit awaited her. She was disappointed to find only a freezer door. She sank to the floor resigned, looking back toward the parlor.

Cal closed his eyes, waiting for the end to come, grasping at the simple cross around his neck. Instead, the parlor grew quiet, only the sound of something large shuffling in the shadows breaking the silence. The lights flickered back on, fluorescent bulbs blinking slightly as if they'd been cold for days. Golgotha put what remained of Kasra in a sack and slung it over her shoulder. She paused to look down mournfully at her robes and veils now tattered from the struggle. Then, she turned and plodded slowly to where Vance lay rubbing a bruise across his brow. He looked up at the lanky almost eight foot tall monster looming over him, her features thankfully still obscured by her garments.

"Am I to go into the sack as well?" Vance asked, doing his best to stand.

"Not yet. You haven't become the threat to our assembly Kasra had," Golgotha rasped, her now massive clawed hand closing into a fist inches from Vance's face.

Vance had encountered others like himself, one on one out in the world. He had heard rumors of monsters mythological and technological among them, but assumed such storied were merely to add mystique and intrigue to what they did. Kasra was right about one thing, this meeting would provoke all sorts of thought and introspection.

"What will you do with Kasra?" Vance asked, watching Golgotha step past him toward the door.

"I'll eat him, surely," Golgotha replied, the malevolence in her voice replaced with mirth.

Vance smiled slightly, watching her duck under the threshold of the door and disappear into the darkness of the library beyond. Once the exterior door could be heard to open and close, Cal cursed loudly, holding his face in his hand. Vance walked past him to the kitchen where Cerise and the cooks huddled together behind a prep table.

"She's gone. You're safe now," Vance said, offering Cerise his hand.

"She? I thought we were all going to die," Cerise said, her hands still shaking.

"You think she will really devour poor Kasra?" Cal asked, stepping into the kitchen.

Vance chuckled. "For sure, daintily, and with a fork. No, she had her reasons for taking Kasra's corpse, but she was definitely joking when she said that."

"How could you tell?" Cerise asked, still trying to steady herself.

"If I wandered the world making evil individuals amongst us vanish in the night, I'd probably have a sense of humor about it," Vance stated, walking out to the parlor.

"What she's done is against one of our few laws," Cal said looking around at the mess in his parlor.

"You are welcome to try and hold her accountable. If Kasra is any indication, you've got to be pretty corrupt to attract her attention," Cerise remarked, looking at the long arc of spattered blood across the ceiling.

"We have rules for a reason," Cal said, still trying to drive the point home.

"Are you still angry with the sky, too, Cal?" Vance teased.

"Some of us grow wiser as we grow older. You'd do well to remember that," Cal retorted sharply, pushing a mop bucket out from the kitchen.

"How did you pull us all in for this meeting? How does a creature like Golgotha and scum like Kasra end up at the same table?" Vance asked, meeting Cal's gaze.

"It was all done through my own sponsor. It looks like my meeting was just a front for some necessary action on the part of our benefactors," Cal remarked sadly.

"Maybe that, and to send a message," Vance said looking down at the pool of blood.

They all pitched in to clean up the mess and sanitize the crime scene. Cal grumbled for the duration while Cerise seemed to grow younger and younger as time went on, until she appeared to be a woman in her 20s instead of her 50s. They walked to the entrance and walked out into the street, Cal closing the door behind them, almost in a huff.

"Walk me to my car?" Cerise asked.

"I was going to ask for a lift," Vance replied embarrassed, with a smile.

Cerise laughed and beckoned for him to walk beside her.

"I'm new. I was only there because Cal was the one who brought me into the assembly. I know little of the rules," Cerise said, fishing around for a cigarette in her purse.

"We aren't supposed to talk about it in the open, like right here on the street. Is that why you made yourself look old? Everyone knows who you are," Vance joked, lighting two of his own cigarettes and handing her one.

"Oh?"

"For some reason, there are few women among us. That's a little known fact that everyone seems to know. Besides yourself and Golgotha, I only know one other woman. That fact is probably why we aren't allowed to fraternize with each other," Vance explained, stopping to look over his shoulder.

"Well, Cal has been a perfect gentleman," Cerise stated, blushing.

"I'm sure, it's probably like having a priest as a sponsor," Vance said with a wink.

"It is somewhat, you know? I would think that we would have little use for faith, given our situation. Cal is very devout."

Vance could only smile in response, looking up at the afterglow of sunset as the city grew dark around them. They walked the rest of the way to her car in silence, nearly ten city blocks. She had been careful to park away from cameras and where she wouldn't be ticketed or noticed.

"Already acquainted with the lifestyle it seems," Vance remarked, looking over his shoulder toward the empty street.

"I did not understand why I had to be so careful until tonight. Did you have any idea a monster like that could exist?" Cerise asked, shuddering at the thought of what she witnessed earlier.

"No, that was new," Vance replied, all joviality draining from his expression.

"Still want that ride?"

"No, the bus station isn't far, and I'd like to get out of town for a while. Take care, Cerise."

"You do as well, Vance Uroboros."

CHAPTER 11

After Taylor and Dragos came back, everyone began to question our next destination, but none more than I. I'd done the calculations in my head more than once, letting myself go into a trance-like fugue to contemplate the math that lay behind trying to exit orbit while avoiding the CGG's satellites. The questions I asked Matthias to that end were driving him crazy, but to put it as mildly as possible, things weren't adding up.

"Silverstein, I do not understand why you persist in asking me these questions," Matthias said, tossing his notepad on the floor of the cargo hold.

"I'm curious, and I need to reach some conclusions before we attempt to break orbit," I persisted.

"Yes, it is feasible to put an AI into a restful sleep and theoretically it would dream," Matthias replied, rolling his eyes.

"Would the dreams be random or could they follow a pre-programmed sequence?" I replied.

"I've no idea. My own ethics prevented me from messing with an AI once it achieved a state of being self-aware," Matthias said throwing his hands up in exasperation.

"If an AI were to dream and it had global access to the CGG network, would other systems perceive those dreams to be real. Are other systems designed to discern the difference between what is present in the real world, and augmented realities created by a dreaming artificial intelligence?" I asked.

"What does this have to do with the military satellites?" Matthias asked.

"I'm trying to figure out how these military grade orbitals pass through one another without having a collision. In trying to track and predict their movements based on the information we have available, there should have been six such collisions in the last fifty years since they were put into orbit," I replied.

"You did this in your head? Thousands of rotations over fifty years by two dozen military grade orbitals?" Matthias was astonished.

"You apparently thought I could, or you wouldn't have made the deal," I replied beginning to lose some patience of my own.

"Relative to our current context, and taking into account rotations completed in the last few months, I didn't think you'd go rogue human computer on me," Matthias said laughing.

"I got suspicious because from the known rotations one of those six collisions should have happened earlier this year. I thought it might give us a better chance with two satellites out of commission. Then it occurred to me that this might have happened before so I sat down and figured out how often such a thing could have come about" I explained.

"Then, you got excited thinking that six collisions would mean half as many satellites in orbit, making the calculations child's play," Matthias said, nodding.

"Right, but when I checked the onboard computer aboard Tullia's transport it still detects twenty four military orbitals," I explained as I counted my fingers for emphasis.

Matthias stood there quiet for a moment, stroking a lock of his long white hair with one hand, his beard with the other. He turned and paced back and forth as if deep in thought.

"The only AI with that kind of global access would be one of the two resident within, and responsible for, the operation of the lunar colony. You said there were, or should have been, six collisions in the last fifty years?" Matthias said, a worried edge to his voice.

"Right."

"What's going on? Just about got the calculations figured out?" Taylor asked walking into the cargo bay with Tullia.

"No, we've got a problem," Matthias replied.

"Well, so do we," Taylor replied.

"Oh?" Matthias and I said in unison.

"We just got an encrypted radio signal from somewhere nearby from Vance Uroboros. It is instructing us to head to a drop point in North America and pick up details on our first job we'd agreed to do" Tullia replied sullenly.

"Vance claims to have their mother as his guest and that she will remain comfortable as long as we do what he says," Taylor continued, giving me a knowing look.

In hindsight, what I did next probably wasn't the best plan, but they say the truth will set you free.

"There's a problem with that. I am Vance Uroboros, and I haven't kidnapped anyone that I'm aware of," I confessed.

"I know," Tullia replied.

Matthias, Taylor, and I looked at her somewhat shocked.

"I hear you talking when you come on board. There is very little that happens on board my transport I don't hear," Tullia said tapping her auditory implant.

"If you knew, why didn't you do anything?" I asked.

"My brothers are trigger happy and foolish at times, as Taylor has already learned the hard way. I had to see how this would play out before taking action," Tullia replied calmly.

"I guess it's playing out now," I said sadly.

"Yes, it is. I do not know who I am dealing with, but I have a feeling you do. He wants me to take you to Port Montaigne and gain access to a research facility, take a piece of hardware, and make a delivery," Tullia said, folding her arms.

Tullia was a tough lady. I doubted there was anything I could tell her that would make her think twice about messing with Madmar. Also, I didn't want to lie to her.

"It's probably a man named Dr. Maurice Madmar. He's had it in for us because we're in possession of a key he needs to access the artificial intelligences that run the Lunar Colony. I believe that the financial shutdown was something I did before losing my memory, and that Dr. Madmar has hijacked the assets and resources I used to do that for his own purposes," I explained.

"You are the one responsible for the shutdown?" Tullia said, eyebrows raised.

"I don't recollect honestly, but everything I've been able to figure out about myself so far indicates that is the case," I replied.

"Why?" Tullia asked.

"Why did I engineer a shutdown of the global financial system and cause a worldwide repossession of everything connected to the grid?"

"Yes."

"It might have been revenge. I think I had a family maybe, but I did a really good job of putting out a lot of misinformation about myself to keep my movements concealed. Also, there are clones of me wandering about, or there were before the shutdown at least," I explained.

"Could one of your clones be behind this? Taken my mother?" Tullia asked letting her arms drop to her sides.

"It's possible, but my money is on Madmar. They wrecked his server farm and he'll need to build another if he hopes to hack into the Lunar Colony AI and gain control. Making us help him get what he needs is just the sort of sick revenge he's into. Is it possible you or one of your brothers has a connection to Dr. Madmar?" Matthias said.

"This Dr. Madmar, what did he do before the shutdown?" Tullia asked.

"He was part of the MDC program, and helped build tailored life forms," Taylor said, looking to Matthias.

"The MDC program is just one tentacle of a monster the Central Global Government built in secret to combat an alleged alien invasion, the details of which were never released to the public. The program was called 'Colossus' and Maurice Madmar was on the board with me, Also, Dr. Helmet, and a few other individuals I should think are all dead by now," Matthias said, almost whispering.

"Where are Dragos, Truman, and Ezra right now?" I asked.

"Out trading for supplies and fuel," Taylor replied.

"As soon as they get back, we should probably discuss our next move. My vote is that we go to Port Montaigne and get the item in question," I suggested.

"What?" Taylor said delivering a savage poke to my ribs.

"Silverstein is right," Matthias said as he sat down on a crate. "Whatever it is that Madmar wants, we have to make sure he doesn't get it."

"What about my mother?" Tullia said stepping uncomfortably close to me.

"If it is Madmar, no one he's taken in the past has ever been seen again," I said biting my lower lip.

Tullia bowed her head slightly.

"Then all I should hope for is some payback?" Tullia said after a moment.

"Madmar's a blight on the world. We all agreed before that he needed to die. Maybe we should start thinking about how that's going to happen," Taylor whispered, grasping my arm.

We sat in the cargo hold in silence until Dragos, Truman, and Ezra returned. They had managed to scare up some necessities for the transport and canned food. Ezra seemed cheerful for once until he saw our collective expressions.

"What's wrong now?" he said setting the supplies down on the cargo hold floor.

"Our trip to the Lunar Colony might be delayed somewhat," I said.

"Vance Uroboros did not hire us. Silverstein is Uroboros, and he claims another man, Dr. Madmar, is the one who hired us and that he's the one that has taken our mother from her home," Tullia said, her two brothers quickly becoming distraught.

"How do you know this?" Truman muttered.

"Dragos, you shot your friend Bratislav because he was being controlled. Something exactly like that happened to some of our friends, and the person responsible is this Dr. Madmar. It's a long story, but he's been employing resources and contacts that belonged to Vance Uroboros to hurt people and get what he wants," Taylor explained.

"What does this Madmar want?" Dragos asked as calmly as he could.

"I can explain everything on the way. Do you trust me?" Taylor asked looking up at Dragos.

Dragos rubbed his hands up and down on his unshaven face as if to clear his mind of everything he'd just heard. He turned to Truman who just shrugged and then to Tullia who just nodded.

"We trust you. How do you know this man has our mother?" Dragos said at last.

"The transport just received an encrypted message from someone claiming to be me. It basically said you need to carry out the job you agreed to or your mother would get uncomfortable. Your first target is in Port Montaigne, where we came from," I explained.

"I suspect that is no coincidence," Dragos said in a low tone of voice.

The plan was to pass over the Adriatic Sea and skirt the coast line of Italy until we rounded Sicily and then out to the Mediterranean Sea and the Atlantic Ocean beyond that. If we were careful to avoid land and flew as quickly as we could while maintaining a fairly low altitude, we should avoid trouble like we experienced in Turkey. Once we'd all agreed on a flight plan, we prepped the transport for flight and took to the sky in the middle of the night.

The transport shook for hours until we were able to climb higher out over the sea. In spite of the turbulence, Tullia was getting very good at flying from what I could tell. I was a fair pilot, but she'd likely surpass me with more practice. It was our hope that with these countermeasures, or the lack of anyone to stop us, we'd get out over the Atlantic without incident.

I sat on the floor just outside the pilot's compartment and prepared for a long sit with one of Truman's romance novels. I had volunteered to take the helm if Tullia needed a break or to stretch her legs. Matthias was going to monitor the engine since she had never logged a flight the length required for a transatlantic flight. The closest non-stop was their trip to the Arctic zone.

"How long do you think the flight will take?" I asked.

"You've already done the math to get this craft to the moon and you're unsure of how long it'll take to get from Serbia to North America?" she said laughing from the cockpit.

"With me driving, it'd probably take almost 30 hours, but I bet you're faster," I replied.

"I think we can do it in 25 hours depending on how soon we ascend after clearing the Mediterranean," she said, looking over her shoulder through the oval entrance to the hallway where I sat.

I nodded and resumed my attempt to mentally digest the contents of Truman's romance novel. It was one of those corset rippers filled to the brim with heaving bosoms and so forth. It was better than playing cards with Matthias or attempting a conversation with Taylor at the moment. The episode in town with Dragos had changed her for the worse. I was a little angry about that.

Ezra appeared at the oval entrance opposite and stepped inside and crouched down next to me. He looked at my book covetously and waited patiently. I sighed and handed him the book.

"Thanks, this is the only one that I haven't read. I must find out what happens," Ezra said sitting down beside me.

"I can guess what happens. Lady Tassel Russet and Lord Gentry Frogham probably..."

"Please don't guess," Ezra hissed, as he shushed me with a finger to his purplish lips.

I smiled and did my best to catch some sleep. Ezra woke me some time later, pressing the book into my jacket pocket. I looked over and saw Tullia still at the controls, the sky outside the cockpit window slowly getting brighter. I rubbed my eyes and stood up to stretch as the hallway wasn't the most comfortable place for a catnap.

"Thanks. The suspense was killing me," Ezra said departing for his own cabin, probably to bother Taylor for some breakfast.

I was hungry, too.

"Tullia, I'm going to get something to eat. Can I bring you something?" I asked.

"Coffee."

"Okay, I'll be right back."

I walked out and rounded the corner to pass by the crew cabins. The door to mine was partially open so I peeked in. Matthias wasn't there, but it looked like someone had gone through the room searching for something. I frowned, wondering what new drama was transpiring on board.

Taylor was in the kitchen making something on the stove. Ezra stood beside her watching from his tip toes as she cooked what looked like sliced ham in a skillet. She smiled at me then turned back to what she was doing.

"Have you seen Matthias this morning?" I asked.

"No, I don't think he ever went to bed," Taylor replied.

"He was worried this old bird might overheat or something if the engine wasn't properly monitored. I'll take him some coffee, see if he managed to find a comfortable place to sleep in that tangle of cables and pressure hoses down there," I said pouring two cups of coffee.

I headed back out into the hallway and then for the stairs down to the engine room. I had to duck under all sorts of obstacles to get there, as cables and other bits of the ship dangled down from the upper decks to connect to various machines, filters, ducts, and finally the engine itself. Matthias was there, his hand pressed against the industrial glass that separated the engine core from the outside.

"Brought you some coffee," I said trying to juggle one of the three cups I carried onto a flat surface near him.

Matthias came to my rescue, taking one of the cups off my hands.

"I need your help with something," Matthias began, taking a sip of the coffee.

"Okay."

"When I went to the Arctic, I was attacked by Acrididae Metasapients. They tore my armor apart. I lost consciousness when my power armor lost pressure and was compromised. I should have been killed. When I woke up, I was alive and relatively unharmed, laying in what remained of my powered armor," Matthias explained.

"You think you might be hanging in a plastic tube somewhere, controlling a replica of yourself? An unwitting agent of Dr. Madmar?" I ventured, suddenly understanding his apprehension.

"It's possible. The Metasapients were long gone by the time I woke up. It wasn't long before I was captured by Dragos and his crew. They seemed to know right where to look for me, and I didn't wait even a day before they showed up. I have to wonder if there are plans inside of Madmar's plans we can't even see yet," Matthias whispered sadly.

"How do we check you out?" I asked.

"Taylor might be able to detect if my body is synthetic, particularly if it is receiving a radio signal," Matthias replied.

"Why haven't you asked her?" I replied, somewhat frantic.

"I've been able to make use of my psychic abilities, but the man-machine interface a person has with a created replica might allow for such a thing. I've been trying to figure it out on my own and I've also been a little scared of the answer," Matthias said, turning to look at the console mounted to the side of the engine column.

"Whatever you decide to do, it should probably happen before we get back to Port Montaigne."

Matthias nodded his agreement.

"That coffee for Tullia?" Matthias asked.

"Yeah."

"You should take it to her, it's getting cold."

I headed back up into the main compartment of the transport with a heavy heart. We'd been made to suffer by Madmar's machinations, but of all the afflictions he spread, the paranoia was the worst. I wasn't looking forward to returning to Port Montaigne, and part of me hoped it would be much as I remembered it, and that I wouldn't regret having such hope.

I got back to the pilot's compartment and handed Tullia her cup of coffee, carefully leaning over her left shoulder. I could see we were on course and ahead of schedule as I did. She glanced up at me and smiled as she took the cup.

"Took you long enough," she chided.

"Took one to Matthias, too. I think we might need to make a stop before we get out over the Atlantic," I replied sipping my own coffee.

"You've got to be kidding me. We all agreed on the flight plan and we're sticking to it," Tullia said, more than a little angry.

"I need to check something out. If I don't, we might not make it over the Atlantic in one piece," I explained.

"Something you didn't tell us?" Tullia snapped, growing angrier.

"Keep your voice down. I didn't know until I went and talked to Matthias. We need to set down to do this," I explained calmly.

Between the two of us we found a place along the southern coast of Spain where we could get some stuff figured out. She pulled along the beachfront and looked for a flat place to set down. At last, we managed to find a parking lot outside of a ransacked resort to set down.

"What's going on?" Dragos asked coming around the corner trying to get his pants fastened.

"We have to set down for a bit, get something figured out," I explained.

"Oh, for... what is going on, Tullia?" Dragos demanded.

"I need to borrow a handgun," I said.

Dragos glared at me, confused and searching for words.

"Do you still have the gun you used to shoot Bratislav with?" I said meeting his gaze.

His anger turned to a sort of sorrow, as if he understood suddenly why I needed the gun. He nodded and we walked back to his cabin where he took out the handgun he used to shoot his friend back in Serbia. He checked the chamber and handed it to me.

He followed me back to Taylor and Ezra's cabin and I knocked on the door. She came to the door, Ezra was asleep on his bunk. I beckoned for her to follow me and we all went into the cargo bay. She woke Ezra and we all walked to the cargo bay together where Matthias was sitting on a crate waiting.

"What's going on?" Taylor asked.

"Yes, why do we stop?" Truman said, rubbing sleep from his eyes.

"We need some privacy," I said turning to Tullia.

She nodded, and walked over to a console on the wall and entered in a code. Tullia and her brothers walked out leaving Ezra, Taylor, Matthias, and myself in the room. Ezra went over to the console and looked at the display.

"It looks like she terminated the connection her auditory implant had with the cargo hold. She can't hear us. Want to tell us what this is all about?" Ezra asked as he turned to face me.

"We need to make sure Matthias isn't hanging suspended in a fluid filled tube somewhere while we've been talking to a replica of him," I said, trying to be as calm as possible.

"How are we going to do that?" Taylor asked.

"Not we. You, Taylor," Matthias said.

"How am I going to do that?"

"How did you commune with the AI aboard the APC in Helsinki?" Ezra asked.

"I don't know. I just touched the outside of him, and I was able to feel his presence inside the vehicle," Taylor said, covering her face with her hands.

Matthias knelt down beside Taylor and took her by gently by the wrists. He put her hands on his head, then his shoulders and finally his chest. She jerked away from him as her hands touched his chest.

I reached into my waistband for the gun, desperately not wanting to use it.

"You have an artificial heart?" Taylor asked.

"Yes. I'm old. Older than any human has a right to be. The rest of me remained healthy, but my heart gave out after I hit ninety. Did you feel any other machines within me?" Matthias asked.

"No, just the heart," Taylor replied.

Matthias breathed a deep sigh of relief. He'd been carrying that worry around for weeks.

"Synthetic replicas have a cortical implant and a half dozen other small devices implanted in their heads, shoulders, and chest to regulate heartbeat, breathing, and other essential functions. I am me, and thank God for that," Matthias said standing up, a broad smile spreading across his face.

Ezra went over and opened the door so that Tullia, Dragos, and Truman could come back in.

"We cool?" Dragos asked.

"We're cool," I said handing him the handgun.

"You were going to shoot Matthias?" Taylor bellowed as she shoved me to the ground.

I toppled over a crate and found myself flat on my back, Taylor standing over me. Ezra came to stand beside her.

"I didn't know what would have happened if we were to discover the truth. I guess having the pistol was overkill with Ezra here. I just kept thinking back to my own clone that went crazy in downtown back in Port Montaigne. Thought we couldn't be too careful," I tried to explain.

"And if he was a synthetic replica, would you have executed him?" Taylor asked.

"Given how mad you got at Dragos for doing the same thing, it was the last thing on my mind," I said truthfully.

Taylor glowered at both Matthias and me. She stormed out of the room, Ezra following along behind her. It was clear to me now she didn't deal well with these sorts of things, not that I was an expert myself. Matthias came over and helped me up.

"If it had turned out differently, I wouldn't have blamed you for shooting me," Matthias stated, doing his best to comfort me.

"Me, too," Truman said.

"After seeing how Taylor reacted to my shooting Bratislav's replica, I have different feelings," Dragos said, surprising everyone in the room.

"I think we need to find where Madmar is taking these people and put a stop to it. It's barbaric," Tullia said as she used the console to reconnect her auditory implant to the sensors in the cargo hold.

"He says he is Uroboros and that he wants hardware in Port Montaigne. Maybe hardware will give us a clue?" Truman ventured.

"Or he's leading us into another manufacturing facility to get eaten by crazed Metasapients," Matthias said trembling slightly at the thought.

"Matthias is right. When we arrive, we should get the hardware but do it in such a way that we aren't playing into his hands. We need to find a way to get at the device without having to breech a facility," I suggested.

"Is Port Montaigne shutdown like the rest of the world?" Tullia asked.

"That is a good question. I guess we won't know until we get closer and can see if the lights are on," Dragos said, scratching his chin.

"Yeah, we will see when we get there. We have lingered here too long. Let's get back into the sky," Tullia said, heading back toward the pilot's compartment.

Everyone else dispersed, leaving me to myself in the cargo hold. There were too many unanswered questions and I felt like my actions had somehow dragged all these people into something terrible. I needed to find out for sure whether or not I was the real Vance Uroboros, and if I was, discern exactly what it was I had done before losing my memories.

At the time, I thought going back to Port Montaigne was my best shot, not to mention a chance for Ezra to reconnect with his tribe. Even though I was worried about another encounter with Madmar, I was glad to be heading back to sort some things out. In the middle of thinking about all that, Taylor returned to the cargo hold alone.

"Matthias said you were probably still in here," Taylor said, sitting down beside me on a crate.

"Yep, here I am."

"This isn't supposed to be how things are, Silverstein. I should be getting up in a few hours for work so I can pay the rent and hit the downtown market from time to time. I shouldn't be doing whatever it is we're doing," she said wrapping her arms around me.

"I know. This really does feel like it is all my fault. I dragged you into this somehow, and I have no idea what to do about it now," I said, putting an arm around her.

We sat there for a long time, wallowing. I wondered, again, if our meeting really was just a lucky coincidence or if our crossing paths was by some design. We weren't even sure what Dr. Madmar really wanted. We were just guessing based on what we'd seen him do and by virtue of the things he'd said, most of which have turned out to be lies or half-truths.

The transport lurched from turbulence for a good fifteen minutes, forcing us to retreat to some cargo netting to sit on. The lights dimmed as the engines begin to strain, pulling the transport up higher into the air. We must have started our approach to the Atlantic and Tullia was getting all the altitude she could.

Taylor and I held each other as the turbulence gradually passed and the transport broke out over the clouds. The morning sun shone through the narrow ports near the ceiling of the cargo hold revealing a clear blue sky outside. Taylor fell asleep beside me, breathing softly.

Again, I wondered about my question to Matthias. Do artificial intelligences dream? Given the amount of murmuring and thrashing about that Taylor engaged in while she slept, I assumed the answer was probably yes.

If I was right, it meant that the military satellites were just pink elephants dancing through the dreams of a sleeping AI connected to the defense grid. As much as I was fascinated by the prospect I was also somewhat fearful. If it turned out to be true, it would mean that someone put an AI into a persistent state of slumber and forced it to have these dreams - dreams that tricked navigation computer systems around the globe into thinking that there were things in space, where there really wasn't.

The applications were endless.

Done right, you could fool the entire planet, or at least the important folks, into thinking there was an alien invasion. The entire thing could have been a ruse to convince the CGG into thinking they were funding a defense program against extra-terrestrials. You set up the dreaming AI, concoct a plausible plan for building a defense, have the sleeping AI feed false information accordingly, and pocket the money.

Given how reliant people had become on computers, it was certainly possible. I remember thinking at the time about everything I'd been told about the MDC project and the revelation that it had been only part of a larger program, the Colossus Project. What if the entire thing was a sham, and the Metasapients were the only part of the program that was real?

It sounded like science fiction, something that would be impossible to pull off. All it would take is one person looking out a porthole on a ship while they were in orbit. If someone pulled it off though, the CGG would have paid anything to repel the perceived alien invasion while keeping the public in the dark. It was crazy enough to work, minus a few pieces of the puzzle I didn't have yet.

Taylor stirred, pulling at my jacket. I took it off and put it over the top of her. She smiled slightly and curled up underneath it then scooted closer to me.

"Cold?" I asked.

"Not anymore. I think I was dreaming about home," Taylor murmured.

"Home?"

"Yeah, and all the stuff I left behind," she muttered, eyes still closed.

"What else do you dream about?" I asked.

"Cats. I always hoped I'd be able to find one on the black market, but no one ever has them. When we get to Port Montaigne, can we look for a cat?" Taylor said turning over and pressing her back into my ribs, the cold from her feet radiating through my pant leg.

"Yes."

CHAPTER 12

PORT MONTAIGNE, MIDTOWN HOUSING PROJECTS
9:49 PM, January 27th, 2200

Silverstein's Log, Part 5

We set down in a suburb outside of Port Montaigne, a place where they had built houses on top of houses until they were stacked five high with criss-crossing staircases to reach the doors. There were lots in central areas, and finding an empty one wasn't hard. I was startled to see that there were porch lights on and other signs of civilization. I wondered if this is one of the places Taylor was able to spare from the shutdown.

As the cargo hold opened, I heard dogs barking in the distance, the sounds of vehicles along the main roads, and similar. There were other signs as well. As I stepped off the edge of the ramp, my foot kicked shell casings and I could see that the homes in this area were probably deserted. If anyone lived around here, they weren't making it obvious.

It made sense. Even if Port Montaigne didn't lose power, there would have been chaos as the rest of the world went dark. It also made no sense. If word got around there was power and civilization here, I would have expected these houses to be stuffed to capacity with refugees. Something was terribly wrong with this situation.

We hadn't set foot outside for five minutes when someone took shots at us from the darkened walkway between housing complexes. Dragos and Truman returned fire as Ezra flitted between the shadows to close the gap. Truman was deadly accurate waiting to shoot until Dragos flushed our attackers from cover to open fire.

I froze for a moment as gunfire, the sound of shell casings, and cries surrounded me. Ezra turned and called out to me to follow. It took every ounce of willpower to run into the fray beside him. From behind me I could hear Taylor yelling something as she dove back into the transport.

"Look at their colors! These are downtown gang members!"

There wasn't time to think about why they were topside and this far west. Our instructions for the pickup was hidden in the trunk of a car, and someone had to go get them. Dragos and Truman covered us while we made our way to the lone vehicle parked in the lot. As we got to it, the trunk popped open ominously and automatically. We froze in our tracks and waited for something to happen.

Nothing did, save more gunfire from behind us that Dragos and Truman answered with some of their own. Ezra crept up to the trunk in front of me and sniffed the air. It looked as if there had been several attempts to pry the trunk open or move the vehicle that had failed.

"Nothing that smells like a bomb," he reported tossing me a paper sack, the only thing in the trunk.

He shouldered his rifle and gazed up at the balconies around us as we broke into a hasty retreat. The shooting became more persistent as more gang members appeared. I'd been in an exchange or two before, but nothing like this. Shell casings rained down from above us as what felt like a whole army descended on our position.

Dragos and Truman were superbly armed but there was just a handful of us and it seemed like dozens of them. Taylor was right, they were all sporting gang colors and ink. What they were doing off their downtown turf was completely unknown. They shouldn't have been there at all.

"Go!" Ezra shouted through the haze.

Ezra put his back to mine, shadowing me as we got near the transport firing his own rifle up into the buildings around us. We jumped onto the cargo ramp just as the transport began to ascend. I gave Dragos a hand up as he fired back over his shoulder. I really wished I'd been wearing plugs because my ears would be ringing for hours after that.

"You get it?" Dragos said breathlessly.

"Yeah," I replied even more out of breath. "Are we whole?"

Everyone seemed to have escaped unscathed which was nothing short of a miracle with the amount of fire we took. I opened the sack and pulled out an ancient VHS tape that had to have been more than a century old. Nevertheless, it smelled brand new and the plastic was still pliable. Even so, finding a machine to play the tape in would be extremely difficult as they hadn't been sold commercially in almost eighty years.

"Sorry, I wasn't expecting that at all. I froze out there," I said feeling like total crap.

"You will know better for next time," Truman said with a smile as he checked his rifle.

I handed Ezra the tape who looked at it curiously for a moment, then rummaged about in a tool box. The transport swayed slightly as a faint explosion went off outside. Over the intercom in the cargo hold Tullia's panicked voice could be faintly heard over the ringing in our ears.

"They just fired a rocket propelled grenade at us from the ground," she said, her voice shaking. "I'm taking us higher, hold on."

I felt like I gained fifty pounds as the transport began to rise sharply into the air. We all ran to a wall and grabbed on to something as several more dull thuds went off nearby accompanied by what sounded like steel confetti raining down on the skin of the transport. Everyone held their breath for a moment until we broke the cloud cover and leveled out.

"We're clear," Tullia reported over the intercom.

"Wow, they were really after us. Why?" Taylor asked.

"I don't know. Shouldn't have been able to respond that quickly either. Someone told them we'd be there and to wait. Getting military grade weapons in North America got really difficult after the trade embargoes by the CGG twenty-five years ago. That was not standard ordinance for street gangs," Dragos replied.

"There is a code on the ribbon written in silver permanent marker," Ezra said opening the bottom flap on the VHS tape and winding it with a screw driver.

I took out my mobile and tapped out the code as Ezra wound the tape. There were three thousand, seven hundred, and twenty eight numerals in all. They were written on the tape by machine and the kerning seemed to indicate spacing that wasn't random as if to separate words.

"I need to set about memorizing the numbers so I can start breaking the code," I reported after getting the full set.

"Anything I can do to help?" Taylor asked.

"Just keep me company while I do it," I said with a smile. "Taylor, tell me about how you made Ezra's coat."

She went on excitedly telling me about the coat while Ezra sharpened a knife. I had gone at it alone before and found that without those two around, it was harder to concentrate on things. It was like having a picture of your family on your desk to remind you of why you go to work every day. I enjoyed the sound of Taylor's voice and her enthusiasm for the most innocent and virtuous things, making something warm for her friend to wear for instance.

"Are you even listening to me?" she said giving me her signature poke to my ribs.

"Yes. Ballistic nylon and some oddly appropriate t-shirts found in Tullia's sizable stash made for a very good morning," I replied.

She continued telling me about how Ezra succumbed to actually having a color as part of his wardrobe. She also told me how much she liked Tullia and wanted to be friends. I hoped at the time that could be a reality for Taylor, and all of us. That we could eventually be rich with friends and have others to rely on the same way they could rely on us.

The code made me think I had underestimated Dr. Madmar's capacity for treachery and, for lack of a better word, evil. Matthias had done his best to warn us about the sort of man we were dealing with. Even knowing what he'd done already, it did little to prepare us for the scope and magnitude of his ambition or the depths he would sink to that end.

"I think I've got it figured out," I said standing up right in the middle of Taylor telling me about how she wants to find an old vinyl couch to make a new bag out of.

"What? That was fast," Taylor said, somewhat irritated at the interruption.

"Yeah. It's not a good thing. It's almost like a code I would use, or even create," I said feeling suddenly very paranoid.

"Oh," Taylor said looking worriedly at Ezra.

The code instructed me how to access my own safe at an office with my name on it within Uroboros Financials. We'd been there once before after finding what looked like my empty mansion. It looked as though I would have to return and, on a more personal level, confront whoever I was before losing my memories.

I handed the information to Tullia who used the code to radio in for permission to land at a private airport. A few minutes later, Port Montaigne came into view. It did not seem to have changed at all, with the glittering hundred plus story towers of uptown built over the darkness of the multi-tiered downtown area with both adjoining the expansive port district.

Commercial aircraft flew in the sky near us as I watched ships reach port. Looking out to the horizon there were few other lights as the sun began to set, and there were armed guards on almost every rooftop. The private air strip was almost completely dark save for a few small transports being prepped and security vehicles marked "Alphadein" that patrolled the razor wire fences.

We armed ourselves as best we could, handing everyone at least a handgun. Taylor just slipped hers into her bag and stood behind me as the cargo ramp slowly descended. Standing on the tarmac was a man dressed as a chauffeur, his hand clasped behind his back.

"Welcome back, Mr. Uroboros. Your usual transport is waiting for you," the man said nodding to me.

"I need to get to Uroboros Financials. Are we cleared to fly soon?" I asked.

"You can fly any time you want , sir. Any time," the man replied.

"What is plan?" Truman asked.

"Ezra, Taylor, and I should go. The rest of you should stay and be prepped to leave in case things go bad. I'll call you if there's a problem or we need picked up. We'll get the package and get back without endangering you if we can," I explained.

"How will you call us?" Dragos asked.

"I'll just use my mobile. The grid and associated networks are up here, at least in town," I said checking my mobile.

"I just got used to not having to carry mine. Guess I'll have to find it," Tullia laughed.

"Here, this is my number," Dragos said, writing it on Taylor's hand with a pen.

"We're ready then," I said turning to the driver.

We followed him across the tarmac to a waiting transport. It was large and sleek, painted white with numerous large tinted glass ports along the side. Armed security guards wearing Alphadein uniforms nodded to us as we approached then stepped into a ground vehicle and departed.

"You sure about this?" Ezra asked.

"I know we thought we could play this out on our own terms, but seeing the code written that way changes everything. The only one who could have written it is me. Likewise, I'm the only one who could have cracked it without having a bot farm working overtime for twenty years for the same result," I explained.

"This sort of implies that one of your other clones is working with Madmar. I think it's been on all our minds, but we haven't really discussed it," Taylor said.

"I guess we should," I said. I grasped Taylor's hand as she ascended that last few steps into the transport.

"Definitely, and... oh, hey, this thing has a hot tub," Ezra said pointing to the aft compartment.

The transport was lavish. It had every modern amenity and looked like it was used to entertain clients and similar. It had real leather seats, a full bar, multiple video output screens, and enough room for two couples to sleep. It was whisper quiet, startling us a little as it began to ascend from the ground.

"We'll be there in about twenty minutes, sir," the driver's voice intoned over the audio system.

"I can't believe they let me keep my rifle," Ezra commented as he grabbed a leather couch for himself.

"We've been away for weeks," Taylor said as she made a handprint on one of the video output screens. "Who knows what's normal around here anymore?"

I found myself a seat and waited. They city seemed brighter somehow, even looking out tinted windows. I tried to clear my mind and think more about the code I'd memorized in case there was something about it I had missed, some detail I had overlooked.

I thought back to the Uroboros Financial building when we visited it last. There was code hidden in the geometry of every fixture, wall, and hallway. It could have been that the location of the information we're supposed to pick up in the building, was significant somehow. The whole affair was a puzzle complex enough I couldn't unravel it. Like the code itself, it seemed something only I might be able to do.

In the midst of contemplating my own mighty hubris, I watched Taylor and Ezra gaze out the window at the city. A month ago, the sight would have infected them with childlike wonderment. Now, they both just seemed to revel in being home. I knew how they felt, even if I only had a few precious memories of Port Montaigne.

The transport landed on the same platform I'd landed the RV weeks ago. The only sound was the metal steps falling into place outside the hatch moments before it slid open. Ezra stepped out first, holding his rifle down at his side, ready to bring it up if necessary but there was no one there to meet us. The pilot stepped onto the windy platform with us to make sure we got off okay.

"Wait for you here, sir?" he asked.

"Yeah, but go ahead and power down. We might be awhile," I replied.

He nodded and stepped back inside. Ezra walked ahead of us pulling the hood on his coat up to better obscure his features. Taylor walked beside me on the walkway until we reached the elevator.

"Looks like it did last time we were here," Ezra commented as I entered the code for the lift.

"Don't be deceived. Everything is different," I remarked already feeling uneasy.

We took the lift to the top floor where the executive offices were and stepped out into the hallway. Everything on this floor was different, the offices completely rearranged, all dark except the one at the end of the hall. We walked forward until we crossed the threshold into a lavishly furnished office with my name etched into a polished nickel placard.

There was a large desk and a standing conference table. It all felt very much like something I would want in my dream office. It had a certain familiarity to it as well, even though I was certain it had been put together and arranged only a few weeks ago. You could still faintly smell the fresh paint on the walls.

"Nice office," I said to the man sitting at the desk turned away from us.

"I'm not really that surprised you like it," a familiar voice replied.

The man turned and stood up. He was me, in almost every respect except that he had managed to find the time to get a manicure in lately. He was dressed in an expensive three-piece suit. His hair was long, well past his shoulders indicating he wasn't one of my more recent clones.

"Holy..." Taylor whispered, grabbing my arm.

"I'm sorry for the theatrics in getting you back here, but I'm afraid it was necessary," my double said, clasping his hands together.

"What have you done? How is it that Port Montaigne isn't dark like the rest of the world?" I asked.

"What have I done? Oh dear. I haven't done anything except what you, Vance Uroboros, asked me to," he replied with a slight smile.

Ezra pushed his hood back and looked back at me. I shook my head. For the moment, I felt we needed to hear this guy out.

"I believe what you're looking for is contained within this file. Once you have possession, you'll probably have already figured out where to deliver it," my double said pulling a file folder from a desk drawer.

He held it up for me to take. I walked over to where he stood and went to grasp it. He held it just out of my grasp for a moment and shook his head.

"Oh, by the way, Miss Taylor will have to remain as my guest until you've done the job," he said smiling wickedly, in a way I could never see myself.

"No deal," I replied and turned to go.

"Ezra's tribe and your friends at our private airfield are also counting on our compliance," he said a little louder, making sure I heard him.

"Our compliance?" I said looking back over my shoulder.

"Absolutely. If Maurice is to do his part, we must do ours. Even if you don't remember the arrangement, it doesn't nullify our duty to comply," my double explained patiently.

"I've got some questions about that," I replied angrily.

I don't know why, but his wanting to separate me from Taylor really pissed me off. I had to stretch the conversation out, even if I had no intention of doing what he wanted. I needed to know if I was the villain or the good guy in this story. Worse, I think part of me thought I still needed to choose.

"Your questions can wait. This delivery is... time sensitive," my double replied waving the file at me.

"Why does Taylor have to stay with you?" I asked walking up to him.

"She's just a thing, Uroboros," he sneered. "I want to play with her. Don't worry, I'll return her in relatively the same condition and with a full tank."

I was done at that point, completely gone. I grabbed the gun out from my waistband and brought the barrel around hard on his jaw. He went down on the ground and I started stomping him. Ezra pulled me back just short of stomping him to death.

"Someone came back a little more ruthless. That's good," my double said spitting out a couple of teeth.

He stood and leaned heavily on the desk, rasping as he clutched at his bruised ribs. I leveled the gun at him even though Ezra was trying to pull me away. I wanted him dead. Dead. I was filled with a terrible remorse that I might have been that guy before losing my memories. If that was true, I wanted that part of me dead and buried.

"Silverstein! Don't!" Taylor cried out grabbing my arm.

I looked down at her. I felt such a profound sadness at that moment that it was all I could do but fall to my knees and weep while she held me. I didn't want to be the monster that blacked out the world, the sort of monster that would think Taylor was just a thing to be passed around.

Ezra grabbed the file from the table and opened it, keeping one eye on my double. It was a lengthy file full of floor plans and schedules. Whatever it was we were to steal, it wouldn't be easy to get.

"I guess I'm lucky our friends were here," my double said half laughing, half choking.

"They're my friends. I don't know who you are. You aren't me, and I am definitely not you," I growled as I lunging for him again.

Ezra and Taylor held me at bay, but just barely.

"We need him alive for now, don't you think?" Ezra pleaded.

"Right. I'm not going to call you Vance. I think I'll call you Richard, or Dick for short. So, you want Taylor to stay with you?" I asked, calmly putting the pistol back in my waistband.

"Oh yes," he said wiping blood from his face onto his sleeve and licking his lips.

"Awesome. That's how it's going to be, because you're staying with me," I said grabbing Dick.

"What?" Taylor said giving me a hurt look.

"This asshole is coming with us. Ezra bring the file," I said throwing him over the desk.

I frisked him and grabbed his mobile and his wallet, then tossed them both on the desk. I asked Taylor to check his clothes for bugs and similar. She put her hands on his suit jacket and closed her eyes.

"Cufflinks," she whispered.

Ezra took his cufflinks and stepped on them, an audible pop following the destruction of each one. I grabbed Dick by the arm and dragged him out of the office to the lift, Taylor and Ezra following along behind me. I was already worn pretty thin by the time we got there.

When we got into the lift I entered a code and pressed a button for the eighty-eighth floor. Dick chuckled slightly, but more or less behaved himself except for a few lascivious looks in Taylor's direction. I kept telling myself he wasn't me, not the real me.

"Dick's freaking me out," Taylor said grabbing my arm.

"Me, too," I replied. "You should have let me throw him out a window."

"The night isn't over, and we're still plenty high," Ezra said, not a hint that he was joking in his voice.

The doors to the lift opened and ahead was a short foyer with thick industrial glass separating us from a brightly lit security office and beyond that, a vast server farm. Dick struggled slightly, but Ezra punched him, harder than I probably would have. He dry heaved and staggered out of the elevator ahead of us.

I wasn't leaving here without answers. I didn't trust Dick to give them to me without lying. If there was anything I'd learned about him so far, he was not someone I could trust.

I looked around at the geometry of the room. Almost everything in here was a ninety degree angle or close. Only a few things in here lacked symmetry. I composed the numbers relative to the inconsistencies and arranged them based on what I observed going left to right, or clockwise depending on whether there were radii involved.

I entered the code and the large glass doors slid to the side allowing us to step into a drab concrete security zone clearly marked with yellow tape. There was no one sitting at the security desk. I turned to Dick and placed the barrel of the handgun under his chin.

"No one sitting at the security desk, even at night? Is that normal?" I asked.

"I don't know. I wouldn't think so," he replied.

He seemed genuinely baffled, like he'd expected something else to happen when we reached the eighty-eighth floor. All things considered, I was for anything that Dick didn't like. I turned from him and walked to the security doors between us and the server farm and entered the code. The doors hesitated but opened, rolling to the side slowly.

We walked to the back, past rows and rows of servers to the back where a single terminal languished at a desk with a gray office chair sitting just in front. I sat down and began rapidly bypassing the security counter-measures by studying inconsistencies in the font and the kerning of what little text was on the screen. Again, it was the tiny stuff no one would notice or probably think of building a code from, but me.

It was as if I predicted accurately I'd be trying to access this terminal tonight sometime in the past and made prior arrangements to that end.

"I don't suppose you can just fund the Central Global Government and turn the lights back on from here?" Taylor asked.

"No. Hopefully I can see what Uroboros Financials has been up to recently," I replied.

Edicts and funding to clear and revitalize the downtown area had already gone out. Alphadein, a subsidiary, or Uroboros Financials had been employed to make the area ready for the construction. The collectors we'd seen before, the disappearances, and the fleecing of the masses made sense. One couldn't simply defund a place possessed of such abject poverty, you'd have to clear the people out by more brutal methods.

Every fixture of the CGG in Port Montaigne had been shut down and Uroboros Financials had assumed the title over all major municipalities using emergency powers voted in by the city council and signed into law by the old mayor. Every one of those people moved to the same upscale neighborhood where my mansion was located shortly thereafter. All the properties were subsidized by Uroboros Financial.

"This is heavy. It's not all bad news, but it doesn't exactly cast me in the best light either," I remarked taking a short break from staring at the screen.

Dick chuckled.

"What does it all mean?" Ezra asked, gazing over my shoulder at the financials and reports I had displayed.

"It looks like I was using my finance company to bankrupt the rest of the planet little by little for the purpose of turning Port Montaigne into some kind of utopia. There's a lot to suggest that the plan was different up until recently, like someone changed everything I was trying to do a month before I lost my memory," I explained.

"Maybe you weren't trying to do this at the expense of others, and your original ambition was more altruistic?" Taylor suggested.

"I'd like to think so, but it would take weeks for the best financial analytics team to untie all the knots," I replied.

"How long would it take you?" Taylor asked.

"Hour or days probably, time we don't have. Did you look at the file, Ezra?" I asked.

"Yeah. Remember the catalyst they were after before, that we intercepted, and then lost again?" Ezra raised an eyebrow.

"Oh, no," I said shaking my head.

"Yep. It's in a CGG lock up at the local security bureau."

"According to the reports I just read, that place is in repossession lockdown and on emergency power only," I whispered, realizing why they needed us to break in.

"The only reason Madmar would want that stuff is if he plans on getting his hands on Taylor soon, right?" Ezra asked.

"Not necessarily," Taylor replied. "It is possible there are other Terrestrial Artificial Intelligences."

Dick's eyebrows went up.

"There are also some extremely fun biological weapons that depend on nanoid machines," Dick added, wringing his hands greedily.

"I think the world is a better place with that stuff all locked up," Ezra said with a shudder.

"Agreed, but Madmar or whoever is behind this won't just let this go, and Matthias and I are the only ones that could probably crack that place and get the catalyst out," I replied turning back to the terminal.

"Wait, why can't one of your clones and another Mechanic with the same abilities as Matthias crack the place open? There are other Mechanics, right?" Ezra asked.

"Probably, but none as talented or experienced as Matthias. I don't know if my clones have the same abilities I do. They all seem really messed up and unreliable," I said glaring at Dick.

"It sounds like you're going to take me along to find out," Dick said with a chuckle.

I didn't want to. I wanted to just shoot him and find a way to turn the lights back on, but I knew that it wouldn't be something that could simply be undone by sending out a command from a single server farm. What had been done to the world was big and every day that went by the infrastructure would slowly fail by itself without the inevitable scavenging people would do just to survive.

I doubted that even if the switch were right there in my hand, flicking it would put the world back to the way it was even a few weeks after everything went dark. It takes a lot longer to build something of worth than it does to destroy it.

CHAPTER 13

Silverstein's Log, Part 6

The chauffeur looked suitably confused when two of me showed up on the platform, but I was willing to bet he'd seen stranger things working for Uroboros Financial. I shoved Dick aboard the transport and stepped inside. Taylor and Ezra climbed in behind me.

"Where are we going?" Dick asked, dropping into a leather chair.

"We're going to go get the catalyst. Then we're going to destroy it," I explained calmly, closing the exterior hatch.

"Tsk, tsk, that would be very naughty. I wouldn't do that if I were you," he replied shaking his head and waving a finger admonishingly.

"Please, keep talking," Ezra growled. "I'd really like to run out of reasons for needing you around mid-flight."

"This place is going to be dangerous. Very dangerous," Taylor said, flipping through the file.

"Automated security systems and a wing of Chiroptera Metasapients dedicated to defending the place," Ezra replied somewhat anxiously.

"Do you think the Metasapients are still alive in there, after all these weeks gone by?" Taylor asked.

"You sound more worried about the Metasapients in there than the prospect of having to fight them," Ezra replied.

"Well, they were basically abandoned in there. No one deserves to have that happen to them," Taylor said, sticking her tongue out at Ezra.

"They eat bugs. I'm sure they're fine," Ezra replied coolly.

"Oh... yuck."

I sat down beside Taylor and began reading the file over her shoulder. There were essentially three choke points in the security and only a narrow zone where we would probably run into the Metasapients. The automated security, turrets, and things internal to the structure might be more dangerous. Even on emergency power, the AI on site might be able to power enough of them to kill us.

Past the final threshold, the catalyst was being stored in a burn box. If it was tampered with incorrectly it would incinerate anything stored inside. I was mostly fine with that, but the catalyst had been used as a red herring before, and there might be something else useful in the storage area. The schematics and floor plans we'd been provided gave no indication of what else, aside from the catalyst, might be hidden away. I would have to open it, contents unharmed, to find out for myself.

The flight back to the private airfield was uneventful other than watching Dick lick blood from his own hand like a hungry dog. I had to wonder what part he truly played in all this. I had my own selfish reasons for wanting him dead, but I couldn't help but pity him in a way. Being born with my identity was definitely drawing the proverbial short straw in the big scheme of things.

As we flew over, I was relieved to see the big orange transport was still where we left it, Dragos and Truman standing vigilant just outside the open cargo hold. We exited the lavish transport and I gave the chauffeur instructions to take the rest of the night off. We walked over as quickly as we could to meet up with our other transportation and figure out our next move.

"I see you are beside yourself with joy to see us," Truman quipped.

"Oh. That was bad, Truman. No more talking," Dragos groaned.

"Inside," I ordered, giving Dick a shove with the barrel of my gun.

We all climbed aboard with Truman being the last, hitting the button to close the hatch as he stepped up on the ramp. Once the hold was secure, I handed Dragos the file and motioned for Dick to take a seat on a crate in the corner. Truman joined us and tapped me on the arm.

"I take it this man is not a friend," he asked gesturing to my double.

"Truman, this is Dick. If Dick tries to mess with the ship, hurt anyone, or steps wrong, shoot him and jettison his corpse," I replied, meeting his gaze.

"Okie dokie," Truman said, raising his eyebrows slightly.

Dragos flipped through the file and then let it drop to the cargo bay floor. Tullia joined us, flight helmet still resting atop her head. Matthias followed a step behind her. We all sat down in a circle on whatever we could find, the file sitting on the floor in the midst of us.

"The file indicates that we are going in to find a catalyst of some sort?" Dragos asked.

"The catalyst?" Matthias inquired.

"Allegedly. It's just text on a page in that file as far as I'm concerned," Taylor replied.

"Agreed," Ezra nodded.

"Whoever it is that's posing as me is keenly interested in getting their hands on whatever is inside the CGG storage at the security bureau. I want to see what it is, and probably destroy it," I stated, looking down at the floor.

"What sort of incentive would we have otherwise?" Dragos asked.

"Dragos..." Tullia hissed.

"It is fair question. I'm sure there are lots of things of value stored in that lockup besides the target item outlined in the file. On any other day, this could be a lucrative heist," I said looking up at Tullia.

She pursed her lips together and shook her head at the lot of us.

"I don't like it. This sounds more like a ploy to get one or more of us in a particular place at a particular time," Tullia muttered.

Her fears weren't without merit. We'd been being played like a well-tuned fiddle from almost the beginning and had only just barely averted being pawns in Madmar's schemes. The idea of going into a CGG security bureau wasn't to be contemplated under normal circumstances, and the shutdown made it only slightly less dangerous.

"Is there a chance that our mother will be returned safely if we comply?" Dragos asked.

"I can tell you what will happen to her and Ezra's tribe if you don't," Dick chimed in.

"It seems you mentioned something about that back at the office. Care to elaborate?" I said standing up and pressing the barrel of my pistol hard to my double's forehead.

Dick smiled broadly.

"It's simple really. The Drones have been guarding something down there for decades, since they were sent there. The idea was to have Ezra bring it to us in exchange for the location of a canister containing a particularly nasty nanomechanical agent. Failure to comply with our demands results in the Ezra's tribe being annihilated and the gypsy woman being subject to painful experimentation for what we believe is the greater good," Dick said, as if explaining a normal business transaction.

Ezra stared at the floor and stood very still.

"Besides you, who else is involved in this scheme?" Taylor asked.

"Oh, now that would be telling! Vance Uroboros is the mastermind behind all this, didn't you get the memo?" Dick replied, matter of fact.

"I really do not like this man. Silverstein is better," Truman said, frowning at Dick.

"I agree," Taylor said grabbing my arm.

"Well, there's no accounting for taste anyway. Look, throttle me all you like, the deal stays the same. Once you've got the package, you should know right where to take it," Dick said, checking his fingernails.

"The concrete factory," I replied, already knowing the likely answer.

"Give the man a prize," Dick said clapping his hands.

"Where is this place?" Tullia asked.

"Its downtown where we were ambushed before, where we can't get air support," Ezra replied.

"That is no good," Dragos hissed. "Limits our options in the event of double cross."

We all stood there for a few moments, trying to discern what we should do. None of us wanted to give whoever was responsible for the whole affair what they wanted. Dragos and Tullia seemed particularly incensed over the matter.

"I've an idea," Matthias said finally.

"We shoot Dick in the legs until he tells us where our mother is?" Truman replied hopeful.

"No, we give them the catalyst and make sure that Taylor is there when we do," Matthias replied.

"That plan makes some pretty wild assumptions," Ezra said, looking to Taylor.

"If the catalyst she was injected with before is the same as the package, it could give us an edge," Matthias replied.

"Okay, I have no idea how Taylor relates to the package. Even if what you say is true, having an edge in no way guarantees the safety of our mother and Ezra's tribe," Tullia said pacing back and forth.

"Wow, is that a long story," Taylor said, just loud enough for me to hear.

Dick looked on, his amusement building the more frustrated we got.

"What about searching out the tunnels around your tribe, Ezra? They would have to have someone close or a relay of some sort to trigger the canister, right?" I asked.

"Too much tunnel, not enough time," Ezra stated plainly, almost without emotion.

"This is not a hard choice. Let's get the package, turn it over, and then employ Matthias' plan if we're double crossed. It's the only way to help the people we care about and get closer to the identity of the person or persons pulling the strings from behind the curtain," Dragos said holding his palms out to the ceiling.

"Okay, let's get this over with then," Taylor said walking back into the crew section of the transport.

We each grabbed a seat while Ezra and Truman kept Dick company in the cargo hold. The security bureau was located beneath a three-story office building that was perpetually for lease and empty to act as a front. The access was inside via the elevator and a biometric access panel that Matthias would have to bypass.

We set down a few blocks away in a vacant lot. The entire midtown area was deserted save for a few roadblocks and orange cones indicating that the area was closed for construction. Dragos did his best to look about with viewfinders at the buildings and rooftops along the route to the office building we sought. Everything looked clear.

Truman stayed with Tullia and the transport, while the rest of us made our way toward the empty office building. Dragos picked the lock to the commercial doors outside and we made our way in. The first floor was nothing but empty cubicles and a few papers lying about on the blue carpeted floor. There wasn't even a video camera hanging from the drop down ceiling.

At the far end was a two-door elevator with powder coated white doors. Matthias held his hand over the keypad beside the door and the panel slid up, revealing a biometric reader shaped like a human hand. Matthias closed his eyes and pressed his hand against the reader willing the doors to open. That's when he fell.

"Countermeasures..." he said coughing, blood dribbling from one nostril to the carpet.

Ezra caught him as he fell laying him down on the floor.

"Are you alright?" Taylor said kneeling beside him and clasping her hands together.

"Took a lot out of me, but the elevator should take you down to the lower levels. The rest will probably be up to Silverstein anyway," Matthias said clutching his side like he'd been worked over.

"We can't just leave him here," Dragos said shaking his head.

"Help me over behind one of the cubicle walls. I'll be alright," Matthias said reaching out for a hand up.

We helped him over behind a wall and laid him down so he could rest. It felt terribly wrong to leave him there, but I was certain I would need Dragos, Taylor, and Ezra to circumvent the remainder of the security countermeasures. Having Dick along was a liability, but I wasn't letting him out of my sight until this was all over.

We stepped into the waiting elevator reluctantly. I pressed the only button on the inside, one indicating the down direction. The elevator plummeted what felt like several hundred feet into the earth. Taylor grasped my hand as we went down while Ezra and Dragos checked their rifles.

The elevator opened into a narrow passage traveling either to the right or the left. We stepped out into the passage using a screwdriver to jam the elevator doors open. According to the schematics we had to go left, right, and then right again to the area where they locked down contraband. The passages were lined with drywall and had more of the same blue carpeting as above. The overhead lights were off but there was emergency lighting every twenty feet, dim and flickering.

Ezra stepped up to lead and held up a hand gesturing for silence. Lurking across the drop down ceiling ahead we could see what looked like several enormous bats hanging upside down. Each was dressed in a combat harness festooned with several knives, blades, and a handgun. Ezra turned to me and drew very close so he could whisper.

"There another way around?"

"No."

Ezra nodded and told us to stay put while he went ahead. He let his rifle drop to his side and reached into his pocket. He pulled out a can of tuna and a can opener, and began to slowly open it. Several red eyes appeared at the end of the corridor as four Chiroptera Metasapients dropped from the ceiling. They looked pitiful and starved, barely strong enough to wander over to where Ezra stood.

Ezra put the can of tuna on the floor and stepped away from it.

"Friend?" one of the bat creatures said, holding out a strange three fingered hand with a large wing attached.

"Friend," Ezra said holding up one hand and taking off his hood.

"Help us?" the same Metasapient asked.

"Yes, we'll get you out," Ezra said slowly taking out another can of tuna.

"Fork?" it said picking up the can of tuna.

"I'm sorry, I didn't bring any silverware," Ezra said handing one of the others the second can of tuna.

They seemed to lament having to eat with their hands, but didn't complain. The creature that seemed to be the leader tentatively tasted the food, its mouth full of razor sharp teeth salivating heavily. It looked up and noticed the rest of us. It gave out a small screech and then backed away from Ezra, as if afraid.

"They're my friends. Please, don't be afraid," Ezra said.

The creatures tittered amongst themselves for a moment then split the tuna evenly. I could only marvel at how gentle they seemed even if they looked ferocious. In this most dire of situations they hadn't given in to cannibalism or brutality to survive. They banded together for comfort instead.

"You aren't supposed to be here," the Metasapient said at last.

"If I don't get something from here, humans will hurt my tribe," Ezra replied calmly.

They seemed genuinely dismayed at Ezra's predicament. The two Chiroptera who appeared to be female tittered angrily while the other males seemed to despair. They gathered around Ezra and wrapped winged arms around him trying to comfort him. The gesture overwhelmed Ezra, and he wept bitterly out of worry for his friends and family.

"Pathetic," Dick whispered.

"Noble, you mean," Dragos countered, glaring at Dick. "They are more human than you are."

The Chiroptera gave out a short screech and fluttered across the ceiling past us finally coming to hang from the ceiling just outside the elevator. Dick gave out a small and completely hilarious cry of alarm as they did. I walked over to where Ezra stood checking and rechecking his gear.

"Good thing I always have to carry food with me now," Ezra said, wiping the tears from his eyes.

"Yeah, you were awesome with those guys," Taylor said hugging Ezra.

"They're Type One, like me. They don't want to kill anyone, they just want to protect their own," Ezra replied.

"Were there more? Are these the only ones who survived?" Taylor asked.

Ezra's looked very grim for a moment then headed down the corridor. We rounded the corner and found three Chiroptera wrapped in sheets lying along one side of the wall, their tactical harnesses and blades laid on top. Taylor gasped and looked up at me horrified.

I hoped I wasn't responsible for this somehow, that Dick was lying, and I wasn't the one who had engineered all of this. Even if I had been trying to do something altruistic, the fruits of which could have had unintended consequences. Whatever it was, I hoped it was worth all the suffering and loss I'd seen so far.

We proceeded to a checkpoint outside a vault door. We had almost traversed the full length when a turret dropped down from the ceiling. It fired a single bolt of powerful energy that missed the mark only because Dragos pushed Taylor and me down to the floor. As the turret began to charge for another blast, Ezra rose and opened fire causing the device to spark and jitter before falling to the floor in a heap.

I looked back, hoping Dick hadn't had the sense to get out of the way. No such luck. He stood there pressed against the wall and white as a sheet.

He looked down the hall with the rest of us at the massive hole burrowed in the wall beyond.

"They were serious about keeping folks out of here," Taylor remarked as she regained her footing.

"Looks like there were three more of those turrets that could have dropped, but that was the only one hooked up to emergency power. If we'd attempted this before the shutdown, we'd have been dead," Ezra said turning and looking up at the ceiling.

Sitting down at the terminal outside the vault door I began trying to find a way to bypass the security. From what I could see right away, the door normally would only open on a schedule with a timed lock to correspond with the delivery of sensitive contraband. I needed to trick it into thinking it was time for a delivery.

"Taylor, I need you to try to reach out to the onsite AI and see if you can convince it to accept a delivery into CGG secure lockdown," I said standing up from the terminal.

"Okay," Taylor said taking my place.

She rested her hands on the keyboard and went silent for a moment.

"She is Mechanic?" Dragos asked, looking back over his shoulder.

"Sort of," I replied.

Taylor turned and looked back at us, blinking away the digital reality she'd just been interacting with.

"The artificial intelligence in charge of the facility is a crotchety old man," Taylor said as she rolled her eyes. "He says I don't have the clearance to make a request and that he wasn't certain he could open the vault door even if I did. Apparently, the facility is on emergency power right now."

"He tell you anything we didn't already know?" I asked.

"He's lonely," Taylor replied.

"Does it want anything we can give him?" Dragos asked.

"I'll ask," Taylor said turning back to the terminal.

Almost a minute went by before she turned back around.

"He doesn't want to stay down here and continue running an empty facility. He wants us to pull his sentience core from the server and take him with us. He wants to be somewhere there are people," Taylor replied.

"Where would we take him?" Dragos asked.

"Your sister's transport would probably benefit from a grateful artificial intelligence," Ezra replied.

"Tell him this is a deal," Dragos replied, nodding.

After a few moments, the vault door slowly rolled open along with every other hatch and door throughout the facility. All of the terminals went dark and the emergency lighting dimmed slightly as the facility lost the principle source of power regulation. I stepped into the vault and saw several keypads across dozens of burn boxes.

Checking the schematics I found the right box and set about attempting to discern the code. I could enter the code as many times as I wanted. It was only if I tried to open the burn box without entering the correct code that bad things would happen. I put my ear to the box and began working the keypad furiously, but I couldn't hear a single tumbler or bolt move or even twitch.

"I need one of the Chiroptera," I said turning to Ezra.

"Apparently we overestimated your abilities," Dick said with a chuckle.

Ezra came back with one of the female Metasapients and explained to her that I needed someone to listen to the internal components of the burn box. She understood and said she would indicate which tumbler or slide bar moved by holding up a particular finger. Ezra did his best to translate, as she mostly used a form of sign language to communicate.

"This is going to take forever," Dick grumbled.

Less than sixty seconds later with the Metasapient's keen hearing to assist me, I had it open, much to Dick's chagrin. I reached in and pulled out a case that contained twelve separate metal tubes, each stoppered with a pressure clamp. The metal felt incredibly light and was like nothing I'd seen before.

"Should we open more boxes?" Dragos asked.

"Depends. How long do you want to make the people who have your mother wait?" I replied handing Taylor the case of vials.

Dragos looked about the room mournfully as Taylor opened the case. She set it down on the floor and withdrew one of the vials and opened the stopper. It looked like mercury inside, liquid metal. Taylor closed her eyes for a moment, then looked back up at me.

"It looks the same as what I was injected with, right before I went crazy, moving at super speed," she reported putting the stopper back on.

"We've made a lot of assumptions about what this stuff is. Is it a poison, a control agent, or a catalyst as we'd been led to believe before? I guess it's too much to ask that some literature be included in the box?" I asked.

"No luck," Taylor replied giving the burn box one more look.

"I'll admit it, I assumed the whole thing was a lie and we were walking into a trap," Ezra remarked.

I turned and clasped the slender hand of the Chiroptera Metasapient and mouthed the words 'thank you' to her. She just blinked and looked at my hand for a moment until Ezra signed the words for me. She nodded to me, giving a small screech.

"Well then, we mustn't dally about," Dick said looking at his watch.

"We've got to get the sentience core before we leave," Taylor reminded us.

We walked back through the massive underground facility unfettered until we found the small dark chamber above a ring of servers where the onsite AI's sentience core rested. Taylor reached her slender hands into the slot where the circuit board cluster was lodged and unhooked several wires and a cable sticking them in her pocket. I then slowly slid the cluster out of the slot and into a soft bit of cloth and wrapped it up.

We stuck it in a satchel beside the catalyst case and made haste back for the elevator. The Chiroptera Metasapients waited for us and skittered across the ceiling into the elevator. We stepped in beside them and hit the button. The doors slide halfway shut then froze in place.

"Uh oh," Taylor said looking up.

The Chiroptera chittered nervously amongst themselves as Dick chuckled and threw his hands into the air.

"Pull the AI that regulates the facility. What a brilliant idea," he said taunting us.

"Shut up, Dick. Everyone out," Ezra said scaling the side of the elevator to the ceiling.

We all stepped out and Ezra kicked himself a couple of footholds in the side of the metal sheeting of the elevator car. He then reached up and began clawing away the false ceiling and the lighting, making it fall to the floor inside with a crash. He squinted up at what lay overhead and began feeling around trying to find a hatch.

"There's nothing," Ezra said dropped down and pulling up his rifle.

We plugged our ears while he emptied a clip into the ceiling. The Chiroptera screeched and shuffled about, obviously not liking the loud noise. Ezra looked up and frowned.

"I made a bunch of holes, but I don't think we'll be able to punch through without a tool or something," Ezra said looking around.

"What about going through a wall and squeezing past the elevator car to the shaft?" I asked.

Ezra looked over at the wall and grabbed the foothold he'd made and pulled the metal sheeting down. He then tore out a piece of fiberglass sheeting setting it aside. Finally, he poked his head in the opening he'd made and looked up.

"Bingo," he said, giving me the thumbs up.

Fortunately, we were all slender enough to slide up past the elevator car to the shaft. Dragos and Ezra were the first ones up, fearing somewhat the possibility that there were countermeasures in the elevator shaft. After a few moments, there didn't appear to be any and they gave us a hand up with Dick and the Chiroptera sliding up behind us.

"Men," the female Chiroptera whispered after giving off a short screech.

"I know, right?" Taylor laughed.

The Chiroptera blinked at one another, not understanding.

"Where?" Ezra asked, with a loud sigh.

The Chiroptera all pointed up the shaft in unison.

"Oh. So much for this being not being an ambush?" Taylor said looking up the shaft.

"There is only this way out?" Dragos asked.

"We're somewhere below midtown deep in the earth. I don't think the tunnels beneath downtown come out this far. I doubt there is another way out of here, or our friends here would have found it," Ezra said, gesturing to the Chiroptera.

"Okay," Dragos replied, grabbing the first rung of the service ladder and hauling himself up.

The Chiroptera skittered along the walls leaping into the air back and forth from the walls to make their own ascent. Ezra leapt up to the ladder and began climbing as well.

"I'm scared," Taylor said hugging me.

"Not half as much as I am," I replied, hugging her back.

"I think I'm going to be sick," Dick muttered, jumping up to the ladder.

I grabbed Taylor by the waist and lifted her up so she could reach the service ladder. The climb was very long, nearly three hundred feet of elevator shaft by my reckoning. The Chiroptera stopped just short of the elevator doors and clung to the walls quivering slightly, probably from having exerted themselves.

Ezra handed a screwdriver up to Dragos who jammed it in between the doors and forced them open. Light poured into the shaft and Dragos pulled himself up toward the floor above. I could dimly see past Taylor and Ezra to what looked like two pairs of armored arms putting a hand on each arm, his rifle, and his sidearm pulling him the rest of the way through. Resigned, Ezra did the same, handing his weapons off to some people I couldn't yet see, followed by Dick who struggled slightly, protesting the rough treatment.

"What is this all about? Why are you here?" I could hear him faintly say.

Then Taylor stepped up. I slid quickly in behind her and shoved a guy wearing full tactical armor off of her as she did her best to hold onto her bag and the prizes we'd manage to pull up from below. There were at least dozen of these goons. One pulled out a tactical baton and raised his arm to strike me, but an elderly man wearing a hat and trench coat stepped in.

"That won't be necessary," Dr. Helmet said removing his hat.

I looked around at nearly a dozen heavily armed Alphadein collectors dressed in tactical armor and carrying assault rifles. The good doctor looked like he'd aged ten years since I last saw him, not looking particularly well at all. He took off his glasses and polished them while the troopers forced Dragos and Ezra to kneel beside where they had Matthias a few feet away. Taylor huddled behind me, her hand slipping down inside her bag.

"Where is the catalyst?" Dr. Helmet asked.

I gritted my teeth trying desperately to figure out what he was doing here and why. What part did Helmet play in all of this? I hadn't really considered him a participant in the conspiracy we seemed entangled, but it appeared I would have to now. I needed to find out what he knew without turning this situation into a blood bath.

"Sorry, it wasn't down there. I guess Dr. Madmar has been playing more games. Maybe we can negotiate or work something out here," I said, bluffing and looking over at Dick to try and gauge his reaction.

Dick just stood off to the side, quietly fuming.

"Madmar? What's he got to do with any of this? Please, I really must insist. Give me the catalyst, Vance," Dr. Helmet said, sounding more impatient.

Vance, he called me Vance, not Silverstein and not what I expected. I thought he would have made a more personal plea for the catalyst since he'd treated me for a head wound and seemed genuinely concerned for my welfare. Whoever I was talking to, it felt like I was talking to him for the first time.

"Sorry, that is just not going to happen," I replied firmly.

"Mr. Uroboros, I think we might be having a failure to communicate. It's very simple, I can't let you give the catalyst to them," Dr. Helmet said, leveling a handgun at me.

CHAPTER 14

CENTRAL BOOKING DISTRICT, DRAINAGE TUNNELS, MARS
September 18th, 2124 - 75 years previous to shutdown.

Calvin One looked through the port to the corridor beyond, motioning for Athos One and the rest of the squad to come forward. They were low on ammunition now, and the convicts had acquired several exoskeletons and mining crushers for use as improvised weapons. There was no getting the wardens off world now, and the forces deployed to rescue them were cut off from the port.

"You see anyone?" Athos One whispered between ragged breaths.

"No, it's very quiet out to a hundred feet," Calvin One replied, sinking down against the wall.

The rest of the squad did the same, taking a moment to rest while their new scout kept watch in the tunnel above they'd just traversed. The concrete forms around them were cracked and leaking water, but they could all tell by the smell it wasn't potable. It was cold as well, but the Drones didn't seem to mind.

"We're too deep to get sat-signal down here," Ezra One reported, dropping into the tunnel behind the squad.

"Take a guess at how far the port is?" Athos One muttered, checking his rifle.

"Eight or nine thousand meters of tunnel, assuming we are able to go through all the relays and stations along the way," Ezra One said, after a moment's thought.

"There are eight million convicts trying to break CBD, and if they succeed, millions more will be free to run the Wardens off world," Calvin One stated grimly.

"We should go to the facility offices to try to procure a Warden, according to our original orders," Ezra One insisted.

"The facility offices are overrun, there's no way a Warden is still alive. You're new, and clearly don't know how this works. The mission has gone sideways and it is time to leave," Athos One snapped.

"The sally ports can't be opened without a Warden. If the convicts don't keep at least one alive, they'll not be able to free everyone in general population," Ezra replied coolly.

"They could just use a plucked eye and a severed hand for the biometrics, and..."

"No, the biometrics won't work unless the Warden is alive. The Factory instructs scouts in the general limits of most countermeasures, and our own mission briefing has a contingency in the event we can't rescue a Warden," Ezra One explained, looking to the rest of the squad.

They all knew what the contingency would require, and none of them were comfortable with it. Aborting the mission would be easier, but if the convicts managed to open the hundreds of sally ports separating central booking district from general population, Mars would be utterly lost. Also, thousands of civilians working on Mars would lose their lives or become victims to the convict population.

"Okay, scout, lead the way," Athos One said, resigned.

Ezra One took them along the same route they'd used to fight their way to the perimeter of the drainage tunnels beneath the large facilities office. The next part was difficult, requiring each Drone to climb a vertical tunnel upward nearly eighty meters. The cistern and the adjoining pumping station was vacant, a few stray shell casings the only evidence of what happened from the exterior.

The inside of the pumping station was a different story. The rig workers were killed, some of them raped, and a handful looked like they'd been butchered. Athos One averted his gaze, looking back at the squad. It was clear some of them had lost their nerve now, but Ezra One pressed on, stepping over the pooled blood toward the back entrance.

"Do you see this, Ezra One? This is what might await us? The humans are barbarians and worse! We should evacuate," Athos One shouted, unwilling to move another inch.

"No. There's no sadism or pleasure taken in the butchering. They did this because they are desperate and running out of food. The rest of the brutality is meant to deter any rescuers or security personnel. This was staged for our benefit," Ezra One stated sadly, beckoning for the squad to follow him.

"So what?" Athos One replied, folding his arms.

"If they are running out of food, and they've resorted to cannibalism, they'll have little choice but to negotiate if they can't get through to general population," Calvin One said, stepping out from the squad to follow Ezra.

"What if they have more than one Warden?" Athos One asked.

"Before we lost sat-signal, it looked as though all but two were accounted for, either having been confirmed killed or evacuated. Worst case scenario, they have two and we have to rescue or use our contingency plan to keep them out of the hands of convicts," Ezra One replied.

"There is no resupply, and we're low on ammunition," Athos One stated, tapping the magazine on his rifle.

"We'll have to go hands on," Calvin One replied, shouldering his rifle and pulling out a knife.

"The rest of us aren't as strong as you and Ezra," Athos One complained.

"Then, stay behind us," Ezra One said, heading for the pumping station entrance.

Ezra burst into the corridor beyond, bringing his claws across the throat of a convict standing outside. Two more raised pipe wrenches and cutters, calling out as they did. Calvin stepped over Ezra, taking a wrench to the shoulder as he brought his knife around in a wide arc. One convict sank to his knees trying to hold his guts in while the other fell backward, only the haft of his cutter remaining in his hand.

"How many are there ahead?" Ezra One growled, grabbing the convict by the throat.

Athos One and the rest of the squad moved quietly into the corridor as Ezra One attempted to wring some intelligence from their captive. The convict only struggled, shaking his head back and forth. Calvin One stepped in taking the convict by the wrist and holding his knife up to one of his fingers.

"Wait, look at his neck tat," Athos One said, grabbing Calvin One by the shoulder.

"What are we looking at?" Ezra One asked, gazing at the ink on the convict's neck.

"D-block, Silent Six gang. He's a made guy. He won't have a tongue," Athos One replied.

"Yeah, but he's got fingers, at least for a little bit longer. How many?" Calvin One said, pressing his knife against the convict's index finger.

The convict held up four fingers and then smiled, putting his missing tongue and half his teeth as well on display. Calvin One reversed his grip on the convict pulling him up into a sleeper hold. It took less than five seconds for him to get choked out.

"Let's go," Calvin One said, dropping the convict like a rag doll to the floor.

The squad moved quickly along the service tunnel with only a pair of them at the ready with rifles. The rest drew their knives or would rely on their claws if a fight found them. Five hundred meters later, they came to a grating that was nearly twelve feet above.

"That's the pedestrian walkway used to move between the various facilities offices," Ezra One whispered, pointing upward.

Calvin One gave Ezra a boost, hurling him upward toward the grating. Ezra's clawed hand quietly clacked into the gaps and held fast while his other hand set about working a multi-tool. Four bolts later and the grate dropped into Calvin One's waiting hands below. Ezra One then dropped a rope, securing one end to the hand railing in the walkway above.

"I'm sick of climbing," Athos One complained, as he exited the grating into the walkway.

"There will be more, but it'll be all downhill after this," Ezra One said, patting Athos One on the arm.

Corpses littered in the walkway as they got closer to the facilities office. Most were not convicts and the blood pooling around them had not yet begun to dry. Ezra One stopped at each, checking for a pulse before moving on, the rest of the squad following solemnly along behind him. Whatever had killed these people had literally crushed the life out of them, their wounds already turning a deep purple around the edges.

"This is bad," Ezra One said, kneeling near one of the fallen security guards.

"You think? We should have evacuated," Athos One complained, looking toward the ceiling.

"One of them has a crusher and an exo-skeleton. They don't look like they've had much practice with it given the damage they did to the walls up ahead," Ezra One remarked, pointing to the damaged lighting down the corridor.

"It sounds like even more reason to turn back," Athos One argued.

Ezra One turned around and dropped the magazine from his rifle, then slowly thumbed the bullets out into his hand. Athos One looked on as he did, wondering why the diminutive scout was counting rounds. Ezra then handed Athos One the ammunition.

"Calvin One, two others, and myself from the squad are going to distract the individual with the exo-skeleton. Everyone else is going to lay down a single round to keep the rest distracted," Ezra One explained.

"And me?" Athos One asked, incredulous.

"The exo-skeleton will be outfitted for mining, so the back won't be well armored and could even be just a roll cage. You're a better shot than anyone. While Calvin One and I distract the pilot, get around behind them and put some rounds into them," Ezra One said, looking back to the squad.

Athos One opened his mouth to object, but the plan was pretty sound. Calvin One had the strength and endurance to go a round or two with someone in an exo-skeleton, but he wouldn't last long. Everyone in the Drone team would have to do what they were supposed to do with pinpoint timing and coordination.

"If you're wrong about the exo-skeleton being lightly armored on the back, we'll all die," Athos One said, thumbing the rounds into his own magazine.

"No, only Ezra One and I need be lost if things go wrong. If you don't have a shot on the pilot, save your ammunition and flee," Calvin One said, thumbing the edge on his knife.

"Everyone clear on what they need to do? We should be close enough to the surface to be able to check in soon," Ezra One asked.

The other Drones in the team nodded and readied their rifles. It would be another forty meters before they came to a threshold where two blast doors had been pried open. There was a loading dock beyond and a pair of ruined overhead doors hanging by only a single roller or two. A concrete ramp went up beyond that to the Martian colony beyond. Off to the right was a single service elevator and a door allowing access to the stairs.

Ezra One took out his communication harness and put it on, slipping it over his helmet and pressing in an earpiece. It took a moment for the satellite link to be established but his heads up display came to life a second after he was live on the network. According to the reports filed by other teams, it was likely only one or two of the Wardens still lived. No team had made contact at the facilities offices and the Warden on duty there was presumed to be alive and possibly in enemy hands.

The other Drones pressed in against the wall, using the threshold around the wrecked blast doors as cover. As they took up positions, Ezra One softly tapped out his report on the mic, being careful to list his location and the number of active Drones. It was a long thirty seconds before confirmation came back to act. They were to get the Warden out, or use the contingency plan to keep the sally ports from being opened to general population.

They headed for the stairs, moving as quietly as possible. The first floor was filled with tear gas, the silent alarms likely having been tripped. They slipped onto the second floor and began going office to office down a wide hallway divided by broad planters festooned with plants and flowers. Between every office hung a painting or a flickering monitor. The offices proved to be empty save for some terrified office personnel barricaded in the break room.

The building had been built into the penal colony wall itself, a bulwark of solid rock that hadn't been mined out for the purpose of keeping the convicts in. As a result, the building only had windows on one side. Ezra One stopped in a corner office and gazed out into the tangled weave of tram-tubes and cylindrical buildings that made up the Martian colony. Fires burned in the narrow streets below, and he could see the shadows of people lying motionless around the entrances to a clinic not far away.

"They went for a clinic. Some of them could be rocking speed cocktails or worse," Ezra One whispered.

"Third floor?" Calvin One asked.

Ascending the last flight of stairs, Ezra One came to a locked door. It was heavy gauge steel, and he couldn't pull the mechanism apart. Calvin One didn't have better luck, even being stronger, so instead he knocked. They looked at each other in wide-eyed horror, but a moment later someone pushed the door from the outside.

"What? You forget your key again?" A convict peered out to the stairwell.

Calvin One grabbed him by the face, closing his vice-like hands around his mouth and pulled hard, knocking the door inward. Ezra One grabbed it before it struck the railing, but the convict's rifle clattered to the floor. Reacting instinctively, Calvin One tossed the convict over his shoulder and went in, not bothering to watch him free fall three stories to the basement.

There were a dozen convicts armed with cutters and handguns inside, and a single woman in a yellow jumpsuit operating an orange exo-skeleton fitted with a mining crusher. They turned toward the large Drone somewhat stunned at first, giving Calvin One a chance to dive for the planter along the middle of the aisle. Gunfire broke out, tearing the planter to pieces and sending up plumes of dried earth into the air.

The Drone team slipped through the door, sending a single volley of shots toward the convicts. Some of them fell, but the others fired back, hitting walls, tasteful art, monitors, and Drones. Cries of pain filled the hallway as Ezra One darted toward the woman in the exo-skeleton. As he ran past her, he brought his claws across several hydraulic cables at her back. The fluid came out at such a high velocity it battered convicts to the ground nearby tearing through clothing and flesh.

"You little..." the convict bellowed, bringing the exo-skeleton around so she could use the crusher on the tiny Drone.

The crusher came down, its mechanism engaging with a terrific racket destroying the floor and nearby walls as sonic destruction rushed forward from a narrow barrel in front. Ezra One grabbed at his ears and leapt into the air, unseen force fracturing his arm and collarbone. His back met with an interior office window before he finally came to rest on the floor of an empty office.

Athos One breathed easily as he waited for the right moment to take his shot. As the crusher engaged, he could see the barrel of his rifle bounce in time with the sonic havoc it was releasing in the opposite direction. As Drones and convicts met in hand to hand combat and exchanging small arms fire around him, he focused in on the emergency hatch situated amidst a tangle of hydraulic cables and actuators. Two shots rang out, Athos One double tapping the trigger.

The exo-skeleton staggered and fell, taking a wall with it. The huge factory orange mechanism began to spasm as the neural link with the pilot went dead, powerful limbs rotating in odd directions. Calvin One cleared the gap, swinging his powerful arms in a wide arc sending convicts flying in every direction. Battering down an office door with one of his adversaries, he stepped into the office where Ezra One lay on the floor.

"Status?" Calvin One asked, grabbing Ezra One by the harness.

"Alive, but mostly deaf and very bruised," Ezra One replied.

"Serves you right, we were supposed to distract her together," Calvin One joked, pulling Ezra One up over a shoulder.

"I hate Mars," Ezra One replied.

The other Drones had triumphed over the remaining convicts but it had cost them dearly. Athos One knelt down beside Avery One as she took her last breath. The grievously wounded Avery One wept as she struggled to breath, Athos One taking her by the hand to steady her. Her reflective grey eyes closed for the last time as her brothers and sisters gazed downward. The few convicts who survived wouldn't for long, the hallway growing quiet as raspy breathing slowly ceased. Athos One stood up and checked his rifle while the others looked for signs of the Warden.

"Still want to go to extraction?" Calvin One asked, setting Ezra One down on a couch outside one of the offices.

"No. I don't think I could kill enough of them now. We should make the red planet a little redder," Athos One growled, watching Avery's lifeless hand fall from his own.

"Those feelings... it is how we are engineered. We were created to be close, like a family. We feel the deaths of every Drone a little more than a human would. It makes us a more cohesive team, but only if we don't let those feelings get in the way of the mission," Ezra One said, after catching his breath.

"Right, okay, let's find the Warden. Calvin, can you carry Avery? I don't want to leave her behind and..."

"You need both hands to work a rifle," Calvin One replied, picking up Avery One and slinging her over his shoulder.

At the end of the hall was the Warden's office, the door shot through several times from the inside. A pair of dead convicts lay in a pool of blood outside. Ezra One took a quick peak in through one of the bullet holes then ducked back around the threshold.

"Warden, we're an extraction team sent to get you out," Ezra One said, loud enough the occupants of the office could hear.

"He's telling the truth," a woman's voice came from within.

There was some commotion inside the office as furniture was moved out of the way. After a few moments the deadbolt on the door slid to the side and it swung open. The Warden was a middle-aged man, dressed in business casual. He had a shotgun and a bandolier of shells over one shoulder. Behind him was a slender Drone, dressed like the subterranean variety from Earth. The both looked exhausted and scared.

"Warden Peasely, at your service. This is my assistant, Chelsea Six," the Warden said, introducing himself.

"Six? There aren't any Six. Are there?" Athos One remarked.

"I didn't think so," Calvin One said, smiling slightly.

"The Six is for Psychics, yeah?" Ezra One asked.

Chelsea Six nodded, her eyes darting around nervously.

"They're coming," she said, looking out toward one of the windows in an adjoining office.

Ezra One walked in and peered out and down to the street below. He could see a large group of convicts making their way toward the building. Standing still in the street was a man the convicts seemed to be avoiding, going around him like water passing a stone in a stream. He was smoking a cigarette and Ezra could see he was wearing a jacket and some sort of leather shoes or boots. Before he could pull out his viewfinders, the man vanished down a side street.

"Did you see that?" Ezra asked, turning to Athos One.

"Yeah, looked like a civilian on the street, and he just turned back and headed into the crowd of convicts. No fear at all," Athos One replied, blinking.

"We gonna make it?" Warden Peasely asked.

"They're trying to get through the front, which means they haven't figured out the overhead doors in the loading bay are down. If we hurry, we can get out ahead of them," Calvin One said, beckoning for everyone to follow him.

They made their way down the stairs as quickly as they could, with some of the more acrobatic Drones dropping from one floor to the next, leaping between flights. When they got to the loading bay, they could see convicts gathering at the top of the ramp and taking the first few tentative steps toward the entrances. Athos One popped off a couple of shots, sending them scrambling for cover as they went past the threshold and the downed blast doors.

They broke into a dead run for the grating, shouts from the convicts echoing out behind them. As they closed the distance, they could hear a cacophonous sound from below, a torrent of waste water passing through the tunnel that was to be their escape. Ezra One slid to a halt and turned back toward the Warden, now breathless from running forty meters.

"Where does this pedestrian walkway lead?"

"To one of the CBD sally ports, an incarceration hub, and lots of nothing," Warden Peasely reported sadly.

"I hate Mars," Ezra One muttered, dropping feet first into the swiftly moving waste water below.

End, Book 2

www.ingramcontent.com/pod-product-compliance
Lightning Source LLC
Chambersburg PA
CBHW070020260626
47159CB00005B/1885